I0450944

The Spanish Connection

The Eneko Sora detective series, Volume 3

David Scurlock

Published by Yama publishing, 2024.

THE SPANISH CONNECTION

First edition. December 16, 2024.

ISBN: 978-1738469741

Written by David Scurlock.

Also by David Scurlock

The Eneko Sora detective series
The Malacca Umbrella
The Spanish Connection

Standalone
The Missing Samurai Sword

Watch for more at www.yamapublishing.com.

Chapter 1 Sea, Salt and Sunshine

Light flooded the room, then a crash of thunder set the windowpanes vibrating as the rain smashed into the glass. My brain registered the storm as I turned over and went back to sleep. I awoke to the sun pouring in through the windows. The sky was blue and cloudless. I got out of bed and peered on to the street below. It looked bone-dry, as if the rain had never happened. After opening the window and peering down the street, I could see a few people were stirring. I loved this apartment in Castropol. My Uncle Jesus had left it to me. I'd spent a few weeks here when I was a journalist covering the Spanish Civil War. The apartment was on the second floor of a small block in the centre of the town, and right below me was the cafeteria run by a lady called Sorne, who also looked after my apartment.

I'd arrived six weeks ago, in need of some rest and recuperation from the hammering I took in our last big case in dear old Liverpool. I was on the mend before I got here, but my business partner George had insisted sea and sun were the order of the day, and Jasmin, our on-call doctor, had put her foot down as well. When I arrived and walked into the cafeteria, Sorne had taken one look at me, then a second look, and then picked me up and kissed me on the forehead and both cheeks, much to the amusement of her customers.

Sorne was a redoubtable woman of about sixty with shoulders and arms that would put a miner to shame. She introduced me to one and all as Jesus's nephew and as if, by magic, I was a local. I had coffee and calvados handed to me, followed by handshakes.

"Welcome!" they shouted and saluted Jesus! Sorne gave instructions to her barman, and she escorted me upstairs to the apartment. Once in, she kissed me again, and then we spoke in Basque, the forbidden language under Generalissimo Franco, and we talked about Jesus and what was happening in our homeland. She had lost her husband in the Civil War and had never remarried, but she ran her business and was the boss! She was a genuine character. I settled in, and my life in Castropol began. The town was on an estuary; on the other side of the estuary was the Galician town of Ribadeo, which was on the border between Galicia and Asturias and at the head of the river Eo. Castropol is perfect for the pedestrian; its narrow streets, inclines, and descents make it perfect for the walker. And being such a small town, it's impossible to get lost. If in doubt, look for the Iglesia de Santiago. It acts as a signpost for the town.

Each day my schedule was the same: breakfast at Sorne's, a bicycle ride to Playa de Penarronda, which was only three miles away, and then swimming, running, and sunbathing. Then a nice leisurely spin back on the bike in time for a coffee and one of Sorne's famous apple pies. My strength had returned; swimming had done me a lot of good, and that, combined with running and my martial arts exercises, had got me back in shape. Erramun, whose bicycle I borrowed, was Sorne's son and a local fisherman, so the fish was always fresh at Sorne's. If Sorne got busy, I'd step behind the bar and make the coffee. I took to walking along the path that took you around the water's edge each night before going to bed. The nights were always silent, and apart from meeting the occasional Guardia Civil Officer, you had the river and the stars to yourself.

Chapter 2 Basque Damsel in Distress

This evening was peaceful. A clear sky, the smell of the sea, and the twinkle of the stars to keep me company. As I rounded the point that looked out over the estuary to Ribadeo, I saw a lone figure sitting on the wall. As I approached, the figure stood up and tried to move but appeared to be struggling. I could see now that the figure was female and in tears.

In local Spanish, I said, "Can I help?" She looked at me, and then, in pain, she swore in Basque. I said in Basque, "What's happened? Are you in pain?"

She said, "Are you Basque?"

I said, "We're speaking it aren't we?"

She stared at me. "I've damaged my ankle; I can't put my weight on it."

"Look, I live just around the next bend; I can carry you there, and then we can see what the problem is."

"Carry me, are you sure?"

I picked her up and started walking towards my place. "What are you doing here, alone at this time of night?"

She muttered something about falling over; she was in some pain, so I didn't pursue the conversation. We reached my place and entered the hallway, where we ran into Sorne, who was on her way up to her apartment. I said to Sorne in Basque, "This young lady has sprained her ankle; do you have any bandages?"

Sorne looked at the young woman and said in Basque, "Where are you from?"

The girl said, "Donostia."

I carried her upstairs, while Sorne went to get some medicine and bandages. I opened the door, carried her over to the sofa, and put her down. In the apartment's light, she looked even younger than I thought—petite and slim, with long, black hair, and suspicious eyes. A tap on the door, and Sorne bustled in with a bag full of stuff. "Eneko, hot and cold water plus a glass of brandy and a coffee. And what's your name, child?"

The young lady said, "Zoriona."

Sorne said, "That's a lovely Basque name; it suits you."

Sorne removed Zoriona's shoe, mixed some herbs in the hot water, gave her a painkiller, and put her foot in the water. "Drink your coffee and brandy; you'll feel better; pain stops you from thinking clearly."

Zoriona smiled and said, "Thank you; you're very kind."

She looked all in; she was falling asleep as she was drinking her coffee and brandy. Sorne looked at me, and we waited for about ten minutes. By then, she was asleep. I carried her into the guest bedroom, and Sorne said, "Do you have some extra pyjamas?"

I got a pair. Sorne said she'd put her to bed and shooed me out of the bedroom. I was pouring myself a brandy when Sorne came out of the bedroom. "That child looks worn out, and she's got some nasty bruises on her legs and back. What's a Basque girl from Donostia doing in these backwoods?"

"She spoke very little, Sorne. I found her sitting on the wall near the point."

"Okay, let her sleep, I'll pop around about 8 am and see if she's up for something to eat, Sleep tight, Eneko."

I tidied up, put the lights out, and went to bed. I awoke about 6:30 am and made myself a coffee—not a peep from the guest room. So, I went down to Sorne's place for another cup of coffee and a croissant. Sorne looked up, "Anything?" she said. I shook my head.

I'd brought my notebook with me; old journalistic habits die hard. And I must admit, I was enjoying writing for the first time in many years—bits in Spanish, bits in Basque, just a few words in Japanese, and of course, English. Sorne reminded me not to write in Basque in the bar—an absolute no-no! Sorne busied herself, got a tray with coffee, toast, and orange juice, and went up to my apartment. I offered to help, but she waved me away. Sorne was away for a while, so I helped the barman, young Ricardo, with the coffee orders. After the morning rush, Ricardo made me a coffee and sat down. "Eneko, you know this weekend we have the big river race; they start at Vegadeo and swim down to here. It's a tough race, but great fun. There are three towns in it: Vegadeo, Ribadeo, and Castropol. Whichever town wins the team event pays for dinner for the swimmers in their town. Last year it was Ribadeo, but this year we have a really strong team; we may win for once! You can enter the individual event."

"Yeah, to finish last?"

"No, you won't be last; you should see the state of some of them. Sorne's swimming; that's like trying to keep up with a tugboat!"

We laughed, but I bet Sorne took some beating. Sorne stuck her head in and motioned for me to go with her. "She's hurting, Eneko. It'll take a few days for her to recover. I've told her all about you; she's even read some of your articles about the Civil War. She wants to talk to you. But be nice; I think she could be in trouble."

I nodded and went up the stairs to my apartment, I opened the door, and Zoriona was sitting on the couch with her foot up. She looked better than she did last night. Her smile, a lovely smile that showed off her teeth. She said, "I need to thank you for last night; I wouldn't have made it on my own."

"What were you doing at that point?"

"A truck driver dropped me off at the crossroads, and I must have taken the wrong turn and gone around the town, I wasn't thinking. I'd been covering a clandestine union meeting in Oviedo, and it got broken up by God knows who? I got hit a few times, but I escaped to the main road, where a truck driver going home to Vegadeo said he could drop me off in Castropol, where they were bound to have some small hotels open. That's where you found me."

"How are you feeling now? You look brighter?"

"Yeah, feeling better. I'm a journalist working in and around Donostia and Bilbao and not very popular with the authorities. I'm pretty sure they want to arrest me for reporting on and encouraging unlawful acts, trade unions. You were a journalist during the Civil War and World War II. I read a lot of your stuff, and you were very honest. And now Sorne says you are back living in Liverpool, and you work as a private detective!"

Chapter 3 The Escape Plan

"Trust Sorne to open her mouth. I assume this was all in Basque?"

"Yes, she's a powerful woman. She picked me up as if I were a baby. I think I need to leave the country. The police are tracking me, but I have a French passport and a Spanish one. My Spanish one has my surname as Zubiri, my father's name. But my mother's surname is Gascon, and that name is on the French passport."

"Well, I'm leaving next week, so by then you should be able to walk. In the meantime, you stay here and rest. Let me think about which airport we should use. What do you want for lunch, or should I just leave it to the boss?"

She laughed, "I think you'd better, and thank you once again for putting me up. You're very kind."

"Wait until you see the cost of the rent!"

I was due back in Liverpool next week, around the end of September, so it should be easy to arrange a flight and get to England. Back down in the bar, people were eating lunch. I told Sorne that I was going for a walk. She waved back, and I stepped out into the warmth of the sun.

I walked along past the kiosk and bought a newspaper, a rare thing for me to do as I kept away from day-to-day matters. The front page made for interesting reading: Anti-communist sympathisers and other anti-left-wing groups broke up a union meeting up in Oviedo! They named some people, including a journalist called Zoriona Zubiri, a San Sebastian-based left-wing journalist.

The accompanying photo didn't do her justice. Zoriona was slim, of medium height, but with magnificent coal-black hair and eyes. She was a beauty, and I imagined young men chasing her nonstop. I sat down on the terrace of a coffee shop, ordered a coffee, turned to the sports pages, and read the local sports news, especially about the swimming race this weekend. I kept checking people for any telltale signs of undercover police, etc., but all seemed normal.

After the lunchtime trade had died down, I wandered back to Sorne's place, and she was in the bar taking a break, coffee in one hand and her favourite French Gaulois cigarette in the other. I folded my newspaper, and she read the article.

She looked at me and mouthed, "Upstairs in 20 minutes?"

Upstairs, I let myself in. I could hear the shower running, so I went into the kitchen to make coffee. The door opened and Sorne came in. I pointed to the bathroom. I could hear them talking, but not what they were saying. Sorne and Zoriona came into the room.

I said, "What's the matter?"

Sorne said, "You've read the paper, haven't you? There's a problem."

"I've been foolish," said Zoriona. "I have only myself to blame, but I think the Guardia Civil wants to arrest me or question me at the very least. I think I should leave and go to England, as I don't want to give away the names of friends and associates to the police. But I don't know how to do it!"

"Ladies, I've been thinking about it. We could fly from Pedras Rubras airport in Porto. We just need to get across the border without getting stopped."

Sorne clapped her hands. "This time every year, they have a big wine festival in Lamego, Portugal. It's always packed with buyers and tourists. You could go next week after the swimming race; from Lamego to Pedras Rubras is just a few hours by car, then off to England."

"But what about the border crossing?"

"Zoriona, don't worry, there's lots of people, plus you have a French passport; Eneko has an English one; they'd just wave you through."

"So Zoriona, you try your ankle today, Eneko. You show her some of your exercise routines and maybe a massage?"

Sorne left to get organised. I said to Zoriona, "Can you stand up, okay?"

She nodded and stood up. I showed her some exercises for her ankle, and she did most of them. I said, "You'll be fine in a few days. I think I should massage your ankle. Don't worry, nobody has died from my massages."

She laughed, "I'm in your hands."

She sat on a dining chair, so she was more upright. I went and got some oil and started massaging her ankle. She bit her lip. I checked her foot and lower leg for further damage. She was fine, just some bruising.

"It looks good, Zoriona, just bruising. Let's see how you feel in about twenty minutes."

She relaxed, and I could feel the bruising. It took me a while, but by the time I'd finished, she had full movement back in her foot and ankle. She looked pleased.

"Coffee time," she said, and she got up and went into the kitchen and prepared coffee. We sat down, and she asked me to tell her about my life in Liverpool.

"I run a private detective agency with my partner, George, who is female, and we get some rough cases. It's hard work, but I love it."

"And you came here to recuperate after getting stabbed and beaten, so Sorne told me. Do you think I could get work as a journalist in Liverpool?"

"Do you speak any English?"

"Yes, I think I'm pretty fluent, and I can write in English, too."

"Okay, so from now on, when we're together, we speak only English, okay?"

"Yes, Eneko," she replied in English.

"How did you learn English?"

"Well, I told you my mother is French, and she is a real anglophile. She met many RAF pilots who'd been shot down and were trying to escape to Spain from France during WW11. She knows the Pyrenees well, especially the part below Irun, so she helped many men escape. And being British, they keep in touch, and some come down to visit her on their summer holidays. And they bring wives and children, so I learned from them as well. In fact, I spent the summer of '50 in Cornwall with one family. Cornwall is wonderful."

"I'm afraid Liverpool is nothing like Cornwall. It's a big, dirty city, but it has its charms, a bit like Bilbao."

"Do you think we'll make it okay?"

"Easy peasy, Zoriona."

So, while Zoriona stayed hidden in the apartment and Sorne got busy with the information about Lamego and its wine, I entered my name for the race. This generated much amusement from the bar regulars, like, "Eneko, can you float?"

That afternoon, I tried the course, or part of it. The race took place when the tide was on the ebb to make it easier for the contestants. That evening in the bar, even the Guardia Civil were getting in on the act, "Not smuggling cigarettes, are you, Eneko?" I replied, "No, guns." They all laughed, and someone said, "100 pesetas on Eneko to win." That produced much more laughter, with Ricardo, the barman, asking the man for a certificate of sanity, which drew even more laughter, with Sorne leading the way. I bowed and said I was retiring early to keep up my strength. On the landing was a tray with dinner for Zoriona—Sorne didn't miss a trick.

Race day came, and the whole town came out to watch. We motored up to Vegadeo in a cavalcade of cars, buses, and lorries. The vehicles returned to Castropol to get ready to cheer on the swimmers. At 1 pm, we dived in at Vegadeo to swim the five miles downstream to Castropol. The leading guys set a fearsome pace, and I couldn't stay with them, but I kept going. It was hard, and I was glad to see the finish. The riverbank was lined with crowds of people, and when I got out, I saw Sorne not too much adrift. She got out of the water. She was a powerful-looking woman. The crowd cheered everyone, and I received lots of slaps on the back. Then there was tremendous cheer as team Castropol had won—the first time in 12 years. That meant everybody was going to eat at Sorne's place this evening!

I went back to my apartment. Zoriona was sitting by the window, hidden, but she could hear the shouting and the result. "Well done, you must have swum well, and Sorne, what a woman!"

"Isn't she? I bet she was something else in her prime."

I was still dripping water onto the tiles. Zoriona came over and inspected my scars. "That must have been very painful, Eneko?"

"It was at the time, but my doctor is very good with needles and thread."

"Eneko, I've written the story of the race. It's in English. Could you read it for me and edit it, please?"

"It'll be a pleasure." After showering, I got dressed in casual clothes because I knew I was going to help behind the bar later. I picked up Zoriona's article; it was punchy, to the point, and well written.

"That's very good, Zoriona. I'd employ you tomorrow. You won't have a problem getting work in Liverpool."

She beamed at me. "Oh! You don't know how much that means to me, Eneko." And she kissed me on the cheek.

Chapter 4 The Guardia Civil knock

I heard a sharp knock on the door, so I opened it. A tall Guardia Civil officer looked at me and with no preamble, said, "Do you know a fellow journalist, Zoriona Zubiri?"

I said, "A fellow journalist, I haven't been a journalist since World War II. And who did you say?"

"Zoriona Zubiri."

"I never heard of her, although she sounds Basque."

"Your uncle, whose apartment this was, was a Basque sympathiser, so that's why we're checking."

"Come on, officer, I'm a British citizen who's on holiday to get some rest and recuperate from injury in this wonderful part of the world. And I don't work as a journalist any longer."

"Okay, but be careful. When are you leaving?"

"In the next week, I have to get back to work."

They nodded and left, their boots making a hollow sound on the tiled staircase. I glanced at Zoriona. She looked worried. I said, "I'm going to help in the bar. Stay calm and I'll bring some food up later. "

The bar was buzzing. I slipped in behind the bar. Sorne-mouthed, "Thank you."

Ricardo said, "Eneko, I will do the drinks. Sorne and the girls will do the food, okay?"

We were flat out, exhausting, but fun. The bar was loud. Team Castropol led the singing, but the teams from Vegadeo and Ribadeo weren't far behind. The drinks were flowing, and the place was jumping. At 11 pm, Sorne called it a day and shooed everybody out. "I'm knackered. lads go home." Sorne and I went up to my apartment. I'd forgotten about food, but Sorne had a large tray and some beers. "Time to eat, Eneko."

In the apartment, Zoriona looked pensive. Sorne sat her down. "Now eat, child, then we'll talk." Sorne poured the calvados. "Let's drink and make plans. I don't think the wine festival trip is our best option. I have another plan. Erramun is going fishing tonight, so I suggest you both go with him, and he can drop you off on the Ribadeo side, where you can catch the bus to Santiago de Compostela and then work your way down to Tui and then on to the airport at Pedras Rubras. My advice: don't sit together on the buses in Spain, but when you cross the border into Portugal, act as a couple. An Englishman and a French girl won't arouse suspicion. Tomorrow, when the Guardia Civil asks, I'll say Eneko has returned to work in England, and if they ask where you're leaving from, I'll say Bilbao."

Zoriona looked to be in tears, but Sorne picked her up, kissed her on both cheeks, and said, "Eneko is a rock; his heart is Basque."

We packed. Luckily, I had only brought the essentials, and Zoriona had nothing. Sorne kissed me and said, "This is your place, Eneko. Don't forget your family."

We found Erramun's boat just off the point where he set off for work. And as soon as he saw us, he cast off, and we stowed ourselves away as low as possible. We heard shouts from other boats wishing Erramun good fishing. The trip lasted about 20 minutes and Erramun dropped us off in a secluded spot on the edge of Ribadeo.

"Eneko, take care, you too Zoriona. Just walk straight up the hill for about 600 metres. Don't worry about the Guardia Civil, they park up near the centre. The bus station is on the left. The first bus leaves at 5:30 am. If you move, you'll make it. He grasped my hand and kissed Zoriona on the cheek, Godspeed!"

We walked up the hill, I spotted the bus and people getting on it, I motioned to Zoriona to get a ticket and then I bought one and got on last. I couldn't see anything or anyone suspicious. Zoriona was at the back of the bus, which was full of pilgrims going to Santiago de Compostela, something that worked to our advantage. The trip was uneventful. Zoriona seemed to chat with a group of female pilgrims, and they wished each other "Godspeed" as they got off the bus.

Santiago de Compostela was awash with pilgrims, with more arriving by the minute, so we had no problem in securing seats on a bus leaving town for Tui. Again, Zoriona got on the bus first and went to the back. I was the last to board and saw nothing unusual. The bus took a couple of hours, and we arrived in Tui in the afternoon. The next bus to Porto left at 4 pm. Another brief journey, less than 3 hours. We bought tickets and sat together on the bus, at the border the immigration official came on board, looked around and spotted us, he came over, I offered my British passport, he nodded, Zoriana gave him her French passport and he started talking to her in French, I caught something about her fiancé and then she complimented him on his French, he looked very pleased with himself and wished us both the best of luck. Zoriona beamed at him and held my hand. He bowed and left the bus.

The rest of the journey was much less fraught. We arrived in Porto to be told the first plane left at 8 am. I could see Zoriana was tired, so I asked the bus driver if he could recommend a hotel. He did, and we stayed there. We got rooms next to each other, and it surprised me to see the rooms had an adjoining door. Zoriona laughed. "This is where lovers stay in separate rooms for appearance's sake."

After showering, I went to the reception and booked two tickets on the 8 am flight. "Not a problem, sir, the bus leaves at 6:30 am." I thanked her and asked her, "If I could make a long-distance call to England?"

"Sir, it may take about 10 minutes. Should I get it put through to your room?"

"Perfect, thank you."

In my room, I opened the door to the adjoining room and called Zoriona in. The phone rang, and I answered. The operator took the number and said she would call me back in a minute. I smiled. Zoriana looked apprehensive. George answered, "Eneko, how are you? When are you due back?"

Chapter 5 Touching Base with George

"All good, I'll be back tomorrow afternoon. Could Binns pick me up from Ringway at 12 am?"

"That won't be a problem. How will he recognise you under that glorious tan?"

"Just tell him to look for the chap with the beautiful young lady on his arm."

"Oh! This gets better and better; did you get married?"

"No, I didn't get married. Let's all get together tomorrow evening and have a few drinks and I'll tell you all about it."

"Can't wait, bye."

I turned to Zoriana, "That was my partner, George. She thinks I need to get married and settle down."

Zoriona laughed, "She sounds like fun. I think, I've made the right decision."

I said, "They have a couple of ladies' fashion shops in the hotel. Let's get some travelling clothes."

She said, "No money."

"It's on me and I won't take no for an answer. Remember you are a fellow Basque, but English only or French if you have to, okay?"

I left Zoriana buying some underwear. I then joined her and got her to try on various skirts and blouses and jackets. "It's going to be colder in Liverpool, believe me."

The shop assistant was a charmer, but she had taste. Zoriona thought I'd spent too much, but I just laughed, "I'll put it with the bill for the rent."

In the morning, I got dressed and went downstairs to the reception. I paid the bill and asked about the bus. The receptionist pointed to the foyer, outside the bus was waiting. Zoriona looked stunning. The Portuguese knew how to design clothes. At the airport, lots of uniformed police were standing around but nothing happened. In the departure lounge, they spoke English to me and French to Zoriona. We boarded the plane. The flight was smooth, and they served coffee. I mentioned to Zoriona that the immigration officers would give her a bit of a grilling, but to just remain calm and say she was with her fiancé, and he'd organised this trip as a last-minute surprise.

Chapter 6 Ringway Airport

The plane screeched as it touched down at Ringway and then slowed and came to a halt. At Immigration, Zoriona had to go through a different exit. I was called to the immigration office after twiddling my thumbs for an hour.

A man in a uniform with his name tag on it approached. "You must be Mr Sora," said the official? I smiled and said I was. He continued, "So, this young lady is your fiancé?"

"She is. She's coming over here to stay with me."

"Do you have the funds to support her?"

"I do. I run a company in Liverpool and have property there and in North Wales."

"And funds on you, now?"

He was pissing me off, but I just smiled and opened my wallet. I had quite a wedge of fivers stashed in my wallet. "Is that sufficient for now I asked?"

He looked up, poker faced, and stamped Zoriona's passport. "Enjoy your stay, Miss."

Zoriona smiled, "Thank you, I'm sure I will."

Zoriona's took my arm as we walked out to the car park. Binns was there and gave Zoriona a kiss on both cheeks and slapped me on the back He'd driven the Allard, a tight squeeze for three. Binns zipped along, Zoriona seemed impressed and let her hair get buffeted by the wind. In no time at all, we were at the office, a quick toot from Binns and everyone trotted out, George, Begonia, Viv, and Jasmin. I introduced Zoriona to everyone and Begonia said, "Zoriona?" And started babbling to her in Basque. George raised her eyebrows and dragged me inside. They'd arranged bottles of champagne and tapas on the table.

I said, "I need to sort out somewhere for Zoriona to stay."

"All sorted," said Jasmin. "Tank has already sorted out a bedroom for her."

I looked at her. She was so much more confident. "And Eneko, I want you naked tomorrow. I need to give you a clean bill of health, George insisted, and I'm not arguing with her."

All I could do was laugh. God! I had missed the banter and camaraderie so, party time, plenty of laughs and even more questions for Zoriona, which she answered with honesty. She had their attention. She even mentioned my effort at the swim down the river, which brought another round of champagne. We were all merry and George called it a day. Tomorrow was a working day. So Zoriona, Tank, Binns, and Jasmin drifted off up the lane and Viv went with them. Begonia and George looked at me, kissed me, "What are you like, another lost waif?" said George.

Begonia held my head and kissed me again. "See you in the morning."

I lay in bed, enjoying the silence. It felt right! I awoke to the familiar smell of coffee. I took a quick shower, dressed in slacks and a sweater. George and Viv both looked up when I entered the office.

"Morning, they chorused." I replied in kind. George put the coffee on the desk and Viv answered the phone. Good to see everything working, I thought. George picked up her coffee and motioned me to follow her to the coffee table.

"Eneko, I need to bring you up to speed. Sugar is worried about drugs and arms coming through the docks. Van drivers who deliver wages for the Docks and Harbours Board have reported receiving threats, but it could be nothing. And I'm following up a potential case of blackmail, but it's too early to tell if it's got legs."

"Jesus, George, I don't fancy Sugar's dilemma, with 16,000 dockers and God knows how many trucks, etc., it's like trying to find a needle in a haystack."

"Now the best part of the news, En, a very sizable cheque from Mr Daud."

I whistled, "Wow! that's generous."

"And today's farming news: wool is keeping the weavers busy, and there are lots more animals feeding on the hills and in the woods. Rabbit has finished work on the barns, one he's turned into a weavers' workshop. And your cottage now has everything! Perfect for that weekend away."

I laughed, "And it sounds like everyone has been busy except me."

"Very true, En, except you turn up with a refugee! Who we all agree is drop dead gorgeous, don't we, Viv?"

"We do. Where do you find them, boss?"

Before I could reply with one of my witty quips, the door opened and in walked Jasmin with her doctor's bag.

"Eneko, your apartment now, please. I've got a busy day ahead, so let's get moving."

She saw my look of resignation, smiled as we went into my apartment. I stripped off my shirt and sweater and Jasmin began prodding my chest, ribs, and shoulders and examined my scars. George said, "They look a lot better, Jaz, don't you think?"

"Why are you still here?" I asked.

"George is the company health officer, Eneko. The scar tissue is a lot more elastic and has healed very well. Your rib cage and shoulder look fine as well. Now drop your trousers so I can examine the rest of you."

I was about to argue, but what was the point? I stood in front of them, Jasmin, very professional and George just being George. Jasmin was gentle with the scars on my lower back and my left buttock. "The skin looks good, Eneko, the sunshine, and the seawater have helped. Just relax while I examine your testicles." She felt around, asked me to cough, and probed a bit more. "Okay, everything seems in working order, but can I ask you when you last had sex?"

I looked up. She had a serious expression on her face. George was trying not to laugh but failing. "Not for a while, Doctor."

"Then Eneko, I suggest you start. Your body needs to have everything working. You can get dressed now, but I'd like to see you in a month to make sure you have recovered. You can go back to training again but be careful."

I got dressed and followed them out to the office. Jasmin waved goodbye, and George and Viv exchanged smiles. "What?" I said.

George said, "Kardomah time, En and you're buying. If anything comes up, Viv, give us a bell."

We wandered out into the sunshine, Liverpool, eh! The grime covered the blackened cobbles and soot-stained buildings. The trams on Church Street seemed louder than usual. Ruby greeted me in the Kardomah like a long-lost son and directed us to a table in the back.

George said, "So what's Zoriona's story?"

"Wow, it's complicated. She's at odds with Generalissimo Franco's ideas. It's a no-win situation, so she's much better off here for now."

"God! It must be difficult to have to leave your home."

"Yeah, it can't be easy, but I'm going to leave Begonia to have a heart to heart, fellow Basque, and all that. You never know, they might have mutual friends or acquaintances."

"I asked Bee to join us to see what she has to say."

"Good, she's always full of ideas."

Just then, Begonia arrived, and Ruby pointed us out. Begonia kissed me on the cheek, "Morning Eneko, I see we are building a female Basque army here in Liverpool."

Chapter 7 Begonia has News

"I have some wonderful news. I spoke to Senor Bengoa this morning about young Zoriona, and he was very concerned. He said he knows of her family. Her mother was a French Resistance fighter and well known to the Franquistas. So, when I told him she also speaks French... He's going to offer her a job as we are getting busier."

"That's brilliant, Begonia. I'll let you break the news to Zoriona."

"Senor Bengoa also said he had a long telephone call with shipping friends in Bilbao and he found out that Zoriona is persona non grata now and if she's in England, she should stay there. He's also been in touch with Zoriona's mother and told her she's safe, she's been worried sick, and he mentioned that she'd be working in his Liverpool office. She was delighted, and he arranged for her to be near a phone tomorrow morning when Zoriona could ring her from his office."

"Begonia, no, that's brilliant, and I thought you were just a pretty face?"

"No, that's you, Eneko, with the pretty face and bottom to match."

Cue more laughter. Even Ruby looked up. I paid for the coffees and took a stroll to the Pier Head. Begonia headed back to her office and George said she'd got some shopping to do. I strolled along the Strand towards Wapping Dock; the place intrigued me as I hadn't known about the Wapping Tunnel from the dock to Edgehill. People and machines were vying for the bit of road that was available. Above us, the Overhead Railway sailed along without a care in the world. I spotted a phone box and rang Binns. "I think you, me and Tank should have a pint later at the White Star and catch up on these rumours flying around."

"Okay, I'll grab Tank and see you around 4:30 pm."

"Perfect, see you later."

I continued my walk. The centre looked busy, and the docks were a hive of industry. There must be money about. I spotted a familiar figure sporting a new thick, bushy beard. "Afternoon, Bernie. How's tricks?"

"Eneko Sora, as I live and breathe, you look well. I haven't seen you since Moshe made those imitation rubies for you!"

"And how is Moshe?"

"We're all good. Business is picking up. The town is getting richer for some, but for how long is anybody's guess. I see problems, problems everywhere. But that's life, no use looking behind you. That's why I'm here. I'm going to buy an airline ticket to Israel, just for a visit, you understand?"

I laughed and shook his hand. He smiled and walked up the street. Back at the office, Viv was on the phone and said, "Just a moment. Eneko has just wandered into the office. I'll put him on." She mouthed Pedro Bengoa.

"Pedro, how are you? It's been a while."

"Eneko, my boy, I must thank you for bringing Zoriona. I've just spoken to her on the phone, and she's agreed to work with Begonia in the main office. Now I have two beautiful Basque girls to talk to. It's wonderful!"

"There's life in the old dog yet, I see."

He laughed, then said, "I know of her family in Donostia, and her mother is a legend, a real Basque legend. I met her during the Civil War in Biarritz when I was trying to do a deal with a French shipping company, a charming woman."

"Then I'm sure you'll get on well with Zoriona. Why don't we have a Basque evening, just the four of us, and let's do it soon."

"Eneko, I will arrange it. Leave it to me. I'll be in touch soon."

It sounded good. Pedro had a lot of stories, so it would be entertaining. After replacing the receiver, I went down to the gym to do some exercise before heading off to the White Star to meet Binns and Tank. I'd just started my workout when George turned up. The workout was hard, the best I'd managed for a while. George looked in top shape and her frame had got more muscular and better defined. We did some hand-to-hand combat moves, and she was quick and threw some hard punches.

"George, that was a tough workout. I can see you've been training while I was away."

"Just trying to improve, En, but I know I've got a long way to go. I guess it's shower time. I can't wait to get back in the bath and luxuriate for a while."

"Haven't you been using it?"

"No, can't use it without you. Maybe later this evening?"

"Okay, sounds good. I'm off to see the boys in the pub and catch up. Do you want to join us?"

"No, I'll catch up later. I've got some more news on the blackmail case."

I grabbed a quick shower, made some small chat with Viv, and walked down to the pub. Maisy was behind the bar, chatting to Binns and Tank. She pulled me a pint, and we all went through to the back room.

Binns said, "Glad to be back, Eneko?"

I laughed, "I love the place, Binns, you know that. So, what's the meeting all about?"

Tank said, "Eneko, Binns and I have heard rumours about a bank robbery or an armoured van job, but nothing definite, just talk. That said, Binns and I started checking out vans carrying money to banks or for wage deliveries and it's wide open to be hit. The level of security is abysmal. It would be a piece of cake to take one."

"So, what do you suggest?"

Binns said, "Maybe we could offer advice on prevention to banks and payroll deliveries like the dockers, for example."

"Is it that bad, lads?"

They both looked at me and nodded. That was food for thought. Security advice! Another line of business for us.

"Okay lads, take the rest of the week to do a proper recce and then get back to me and we'll develop a plan and see if it looks worthwhile."

We chatted for a while. Tank said the warehouse was busy. The lads working there were a dependable group, and with Pedro Bengoa operating it, things were on organised. Jasmin loved her work at the hospital, and she'd even started a group therapy session for people with addictions. Binns was working more with him, apart from his occasional visit to Wales, where things were going from strength to strength. So, all good.

I wandered back to the office in a thoughtful mood, plenty of things to get my teeth into. At the office Viv had gone and George had got the bath going, Begonia had rung and said she was going to give it a miss as she had things to talk over with Zoriona. I got undressed and washed and shampooed myself and then lowered my body into the water. Wow! My scars started throbbing! I heard George come into the office; she'd gone back to her place for some clothes. She got undressed and washed herself. I looked her over. She was looking like a real athlete, honed and muscular. "You're looking in shape, George."

"Do you reckon? I must admit I've been training hard, don't want to let you down."

"George, you could never let me down, you know that. Now, what's this blackmail business about?"

"It's intriguing. The person concerned is a female barrister who is married to a doctor, an expert in infectious diseases. They have been married for 15 years, no kids. He plays away from time to time. The barrister also plays away but only with women, and the husband knows. The barrister has an ongoing affair with her private secretary, and it was all under wraps until three weeks ago. Both she and the secretary went to a function at the town hall for a charity event and because they'd be eating and drinking, they booked a room at the Adelphi. Then in the morning, they could throw off the glad rags and put on the working gear and go to the office.

However, during the evening, a delightful young lady at their table started flirting with them and when the evening ended and by now, they'd had more than a few drinks, they shared a taxi to the Adelphi where the young lady was also staying. She invited them to her room for a drink, which was on the same floor as theirs. They had a couple more drinks, inhibitions went out of the window, so things got passionate, and it ended up being a threesome. The barrister said when she woke up in the morning, the young lady was still there, but dressed in a business suit, she kissed them both goodbye, said she'd had a memorable night, but had to run. The London train was leaving at 8 am. She left her business card for them. The barrister said she felt quite hungover, as did the secretary, so they went back to their room, showered, dressed, and went down to breakfast. Over breakfast, the secretary mentioned she was gob smacked they'd got involved in a threesome, but the young lady was gorgeous! So, they just laughed it off and put it down to the booze and, being adventurous, it had spiced up their love life."

"That's it, who's blackmailing who?"

"That's just it, nobody at present, except that a large brown envelope arrived at their office about three weeks after later with photos of the three of them in various poses, and this is going to sound familiar, some of them having sex with two men, although only the men's torsos are in the photos."

"But no demands?"

"No, but she is a barrister, so there must be some reason behind it."

"I agree. We need to keep a close watch on it. How is the barrister, shocked, angry?"

"I think she was shocked, but she seems more perplexed now, maybe bewildered."

"Yeah, it must have cost money. Did the lady's business card check out?"

"Non-existent address and phone number."

"She must trust you, George?"

"She went to school with Rhian in Chester, hence the connection."

"Your name must be getting around far and wide."

She gave me full eyebrow treatment for that remark. Time to exit the bath while still in one piece.

In my apartment I heard the doorbell ring, but George sang out, "I've got it En."

I heard laughter. I could hear Begonia with Zoriona, Jasmin, and Viv. Begonia was showing them some of her sketches she'd done over the summer of the washerwomen. They were excellent. Jasmin and Zoriona loved them.

Begonia said, "I want to do a group one of all you girls tonight! Jasmin and Zoriona looked at me and I said, "I'm off to the pub. "

Begonia shouted, "Don't worry, you'll see the finished sketch."

Chapter 8 Old flame

The night air chilled the body, but it didn't have the proper bite of the coming winter. I decided against the White Star and my feet seemed to have a life of their own as they dragged me to the Adelphi. The evening traffic had just gone, and the trams were half empty. People were walking and talking about the latest films and making their way to the cinema. The Adelphi was lit up as usual, creating a very enticing atmosphere. In the bar, I ordered a rum and wandered over to a table in the so I could people watch in comfort. The bar filled up, some business type staying over for the night and a few local couples enjoying the dying embers of the Indian summer. I was enjoying myself, guessing the occupations of the people thronging the bar. After ordering a refill, I continued with my pastime when I recognised Jackie, who was with a beautiful lady. I hadn't seen her since we finished the case in which Charlotte died. It had been quite a while; she hadn't seen me. The friend she was with was taken with her; Jackie was still making a living at what she did best.

Then it hit me. If anyone knew who the girl George was looking for, it had to be Jackie. Jackie and her friend wandered off, and I finished my drink and walked back to the White Star, ordered brandy from Maggie and I rang the office.

George answered, "Is it safe to return?"

George laughed, "Yes, they've all gone. I'm just tidying up."

"Wait for me. I've got an idea I want to talk about with you. See you in a minute."

I waved to Maggie and walked up the lane. George had the office door open. "How did the sketching go?"

"Very well, Bee is getting very professional. She's got the main outline done. It'll look terrific when she's finished. Zoriona naked is delicious! What have you got on your mind?"

"I strolled up to the Adelphi for a drink and I was doing my usual people watching when Jackie arrived with another woman. And I thought if anybody knew your barrister's blackmailer, it would be Jackie."

"En, that's brilliant. I'll give her a bell tomorrow. Okay En, I'm off to bed, 7 am in the gym, okay?"

"See you there."

I read for a while and then turned in. George's morning knock on my door came with the message, "See you downstairs."

"Let's do it, George."

We went at it for about an hour, then George said, "That's me. I'll get a quick shower and see you for coffee."

I nodded and finished with some squats and push-ups. After showering, I dressed in black cord trousers and a matching black sweater. The smell of coffee hit me as I entered the office. George shouted, "Toast?"

"Sounds good."

Viv was typing away and little Helen was sitting at the low table drawing. I looked at Viv. She mouthed, "She's not feeling well." I looked at the drawing. "Hey that's good, Helen, is it George?"

Helen nodded. George put my coffee and toast on the table and said, "Leave Helen to it, she's wants to finish it today because she's back at school tomorrow."

I nodded and drank my coffee and ate my toast. I felt like we were all waiting for something to happen. I'd had enough of recuperating. Action was required. The phone rang. Viv answered, "George, it's for you."

George took the call and looked surprised but carried on with the conversation, but she looked over at me and raised those eyebrows and came and sat next to me. The conversation went on for quite a while, with George being both sympathetic and dogmatic.

George put the phone down. "Let's talk in the apartment."

She smiled at Viv and pointed at Helen. Viv nodded and carried on with her typing. Viv shouted, "I'll put some more coffee on."

We sat down in my apartment. George laughed and said, "Life never ceases to surprise me. You remember the barrister and her secretary had that lustful evening in the Adelphi, well it seems the whole affair has aroused the secretary's sexual curiosity somewhat."

"I thought it would have scared her for life."

"Quite the opposite, it would appear. She ran into an old school friend, and they got talking. She knew her friend shared similar interests, but she was stunned when her friend invited her to an all-girls' party. Everybody masked, so no names, no pack drill over at a house in Chester. Our secretary didn't know what to do, but curiosity got the best of her and off she went, dressed for the part with a duffle coat covering it all. At the house, she dropped her duffel coat off at the cloakroom before going into the main room. She reckoned there were twenty naked women there, all masked. She said she amazed herself by getting into the spirit of things and taking part in liaisons going on all over the place. Then it got interesting. A woman was stooping when she saw the tattoo on her right buttock. It belonged to the lady at the Adelphi. She didn't know what to do but made sure she stayed well away from her during the evening. Near the end of the evening, she went to the bathroom and while there, she heard women coming in. One of them said, "Stacey Michel, I'd recognise that arse anywhere, especially with that tattoo on it."

The other woman laughed and said, "Mum's the word or I'll get going with my dominatrix act."

The secretary didn't move for about ten minutes and then said her goodbyes and drove home, and she hadn't mentioned it to her boss, she's worried she'll get fired.

"Now this is getting interesting. We need to get in touch with Jackie. I wonder who she would prefer to spill the beans to, you or me?"

"En, it has to be you. She fancies you and you know maybe..."

"George," I stopped what I was going to say.

George looked me over. "Chicken, and I'll tell Dr Jasmin you refused her medical advice. I'll ring Jackie. I know we've got her number, and I'll book you a room in the Adelphi."

And before I could protest, she'd gone back into the office and was whispering to Viv and making a phone call. "Jackie, it's George. How are you? Me, all good, thanks. Listen, Eneko wants to talk to you about a case he's investigating. How are you fixed for a meeting tonight? Brilliant, say 8 pm at the cocktail bar in the Adelphi? Is he what? Lacking TLC, oh, I'm sure of it. See you, bye."

Viv laughed and mouthed, "Boss, your business partner is pimping you out."

George winked. "For God and company. Oh, and En, put it down on expenses."

I put on my best pissed off look and said, "I need the company of men" and waltzed off to the Kardomah. Ruby walked me to my favourite table near the back and brought me over a coffee. "You look put out, En. What's up?"

"Nothing Ruby, just trying to get used to our wonderful Liverpool weather again."

She laughed. "Enjoy before the fog comes creeping back."

I was enjoying my coffee without being mithered. Suddenly, there was a commotion at the door. I looked up and Ruby came over. "A gang has just knocked off the Docks and Harbours wages van. They blocked off Castle Street and took off down Harrington Street and disappeared."

The phone rang. Ruby picked it up. "Yeah, En's having a coffee," and handed me the phone. "It's Tank."

"Eneko, I'm with Binns. Looks like we were on the money about that wage robbery. Do we contact the Docks and Harbours Board and suggest we sort it out for them?"

"Not yet. Let it fester for a while. I'll give Sugar a day or so and then see what he's got to say. You never know, it may just be straight forward."

"Okay Eneko, anything else?"

"Not for today. I'll contact Sugar tomorrow, but I think he's more worried about drugs and arms coming through the docks. Let's catch up tomorrow night and I'll bring you up to date."

Ruby said, "En, you've got company."

Begonia and Zoriona came over and sat down with me. I ordered more coffee and some scones. The girls looked to be in a good mood. Zoriona appeared calmer, more relaxed.

"How's the new job, Zoriona?"

"It's superb. Begonia has been wonderful, and Pedro is an absolute gentleman, but he can be strict."

I raised my eyebrows.

"No Basque in the office unless it's a client. Otherwise, it's English or French."

I laughed. "He's making sure you get to know Liverpool life as soon as possible."

Begonia jumped up. "I've got to go to one of my arts classes. It starts in ten minutes. See you tonight."

"I'm glad I bumped into you today, Zoriona. I've got an idea of how you could start doing some writing. Now in Liverpool, drugs are the big thing, lots of illegal imports. Maybe you could do a story and tie it up with where the shipments come from in Europe. If it isn't Amsterdam, it's southern Europe. Do you have contacts in France and Spain?"

"Are you trying to keep me busy, Eneko? But that's a great idea. I have contacts in France and Spain, of course, but also in Italy. My Italian is pretty good, too."

"Well, I'm pretty sure there's going to be a big drug operation in Liverpool soon. If you do some background work in Europe, I'll try to get some specific information here in Liverpool."

"Okay, that becomes my new hobby, good I'll get to work."

Chapter 9 Viv panics

I paid and went back to the office. I was happy to see how well Zoriona was enjoying life in Liverpool. She looked happy, which was the most important thing. After many attempts at ringing Sorne, I'd got through and thanked her for looking after us. She sounded pleased to hear from me and told me to keep in touch. I walked into the office and George was on the phone and Viv was standing there looking a mite frantic.

George put the phone down. "That was the hospital. Frank is going to be okay, just a mild stroke."

Viv swayed, and I caught her and put her on the couch. George took charge. "En, pour a Remy and make a coffee, please."

I complied and George was talking to Viv. The phone rang. Jasmin said, "Eneko, can you put George on, please?"

"Hi Jazz, how is he?"

George listened then put the phone down and said, "Frank is going to be in hospital for a couple of weeks and then when he gets out, he won't be able to do the job he's doing now or climb those three flights of stairs to his flat above the cooperage either."

"What am I going to do with him?" sniffled Viv.

The door opened and in walked Binns, he walked over to Viv and gave her a hug and a kiss on the cheek.

George winked at me.

Binns said, "Tank, and I have been talking to Frank for a while about taking over his cooperage as an extension to the warehouse, as we need the space. I'll tell him not to worry, we'll sort it out. The rent is not a problem, and we'll turn his office into a flat, so he doesn't have to climb those bloody stairs. I'll get on it right away if you think he'll agree?"

"He'll agree, I'll see to that," said Viv.

Binns said, "Right!" Picked up the phone and arranged for Tank and a team of decorators to meet him at the cooper's yard later this afternoon. Binns kissed Viv and shot off.

Viv went crimson and George picked her up, kissed her on the forehead and each cheek and said, "Good choice. Now let's get down to the hospital. And you, En, make sure you do the business tonight. We need that information. And can you hold the fort until 4 pm?"

I nodded. I sat down and drank a Remy, what a day and it was only going to get more complicated. All quiet in the office and spot on four pm, George walked in. "Vee has gone home, and she picked the kids up from school. She spoke to Frank, and he agreed. He's still weak, but Jazz reckons he should make a full recovery and Frank's doctor agreed. Binns, who'd have thought?"

"Well, it makes sense, young woman with two kids and Binns, a man in his prime with property in Wales."

"You make it sound like anyone who has property in Wales is a catch."

"It's true, there's you, Begonia, Binns, and Rabbit."

"Don't forget yourself, Eneko Sora."

I laughed, "Yeah, me too. But now there's tonight! I wonder if Jackie knows our Stacey Michel?"

George laughed, "Why don't you have a workout? I'll put on the bath."

I worked out for about an hour. I was quite pleased at how my speed was improving and my strength, too. Upstairs, George was already in the bath. So I got washed and joined her.

George said, "You need to impress and remember to stay focussed. Forget the Eneko, I love a man with firm buttocks until you have all the dirt and then she can inspect your perfect rear end. I must admit, it looks firm."

"Enough, George. Have you thought of questions I need to ask Jackie?"

"No, just keep it simple. I'm sure she'll get distracted."

I growled as I got out of the bath. George was still laughing. In my apartment, hanging up, was my navy-blue suit, pale blue shirt, matching socks and tie and my new black shoes. After dressing, I went back into the office. George was sitting at the desk. She said, "Give us a twirl, En? You'll do, and I'll see you in one piece in the morning."

The evening had brought a chill to the air. The streets were empty. The workers had left for the night. The only noise was the rumble of trams and the slamming of taxi doors. A couple of drunks looking much the worse for wear, and a few kids were sitting outside the pub on Victoria Street. The kids waiting for their fathers or mothers to give them a packet of crisps, the drunks oblivious. I walked on by heading for the affluence of the Adelphi, thanking my lucky stars. The cocktail bar looked inviting. I ordered a dry, cold sherry. No Jackie, I assumed she'd be late, until a hand squeezed my buttocks. I turned. Jackie kissed me on the cheek. "You're looking good, Eneko."

I said, "So are you, Jackie, it's been a while. Drink?"

"I'll have the same, thanks."

The barman placed two more on the bar. "Are you going to stay at the bar, or should I send them over to a table?"

"That's an idea. Can you place us in the corner?"

"Sir."

Jackie and I moved over to the table and a waitress brought over the drinks. We sat down. Jackie smiled. She looked terrific, a nice cocktail dress in midnight blue with matching accessories. She looked dressed to kill.

"So Eneko, what's this case you're working on, full of intrigue and murder, most foul?"

I laughed, "No, just a routine case of blackmail, something quite normal?"

"Oh! How boring and I was getting all worked up."

"Are you hungry?"

"No, but another drink would go down well, champagne perhaps?"
I called the waitress and placed the order and added a few nibbles.
"So Eneko, I'm all ears!"

"Well, it's pretty complicated, but do you know Stacey Michel?"

"Stacey Michel! Jesus Eneko, she's terrible news. She looks like butter wouldn't melt in her mouth, but she's a genuine horror. She's into everything, including being a dominatrix for both male and female clients."

"So, she's got a reputation, then?"

"And some? What's she done now?"

"I'm not sure, but it won't be pretty."

"Well, Eneko, her usual scam is, pick up the client, get them into her room, fix him or her a Mickey Finn and bob's your uncle. Compromising photos follow later. They're clever though, they only ask for enough money, not too much so the client doesn't go to the police. Saying that I haven't seen her for a while, I heard she was working in Manchester and Chester."

"Which blokes does she work with?"

Chapter 10 Sugar has some answers

"A couple of real scum bags, real nasty bastards. One of them tried it on with me one night, but the barman distracted him, and I beat it."

"Do these charming chaps have names?"

"I'll tell you in your room, these walls have ears."

After paying for the drinks, we drifted upstairs to the room George had booked. We entered the room. Jackie smiled and said, "You said you only wanted to ask me questions, didn't you?"

She excused herself and went to the bathroom. All I could hear was the sound of running water and then Jackie reappeared naked, "I'll take payment for tonight's information in bed with you, so get naked."

As I stripped off, Jackie looked at the scars on my chest and shoulder and the one on my buttocks. She looked at it, "Who did this to your arse? I'll kill them."

We laughed and jumped into bed, but only after she turned off the light. I awoke, it was six, Jackie was awake and standing at the end of the bed. "Time for a little more TLC. I don't get to see you very often, so I'm going to make the most of this."

I showered and got dressed. Jackie had already gone after flattering me to the nth degree. She said if she had any more information, she'd be in touch, and again she warned me to be careful. She'd left a note with two names on it. I didn't know either of them. After I walked back to the office; I was dying for one of George's coffees and a bacon sandwich. Viv looked up as I walked in.

"Any news on Frank, Viv?"

Hi boss, "Yeah, I rang earlier. He's okay, but he's got to stay in for a while, for how long they didn't say. I'll put the coffee on."

"Thanks, I'll just get changed." I went in and got changed and came back out to find George with a bag of shopping.

"Hungry En? I'm just about to put some bacon on. Fancy a sandwich? You must be hungry after your exertions last night."

I put on my best smile. "Thanks George, I'm starving."

Viv and George exchanged looks and then Viv got back to typing. The coffee hit the spot, and so did the bacon sandwich.

George said, "Do we need to catch up on any new information?"

"Yeah, we do."

We went and sat on the sofa. I showed the note with the names on it to George. She shook her head. I then explained what Jackie had told me about Stacey Michel. Those famous eyebrows furrowed.

"So, it's got to be the right woman. We need to find out who these guys are, fast. Would Sugar know, En?"

"I'm hoping he does, but I'd like to know what they have in mind for our barrister friend."

George looked at me and said, "You look like the cat who just got the cream." Do I need to call Doctor Jazz to see if everything is in full working order?"

"I have a witness who can speak on my behalf."

"Oh, excuse me, look who's pleased with himself. She kissed me on the cheek. It's good to see you more like your old self. You ring, Sugar."

I rang Sugar. "How's it going, busy?"

"Up to my neck in it. What's up?"

"Do you know Billy Ashurst and Brian Godfrey?"

"Jesus Eneko, you always come up with some real prize dead shits. The pair of them are bad news, photos of people in compromising situations and then money changes hands, but nothing ever comes our way, so if you nail them, I'll see you get a reward. They have a boss called Barry Whitehead, and the trollop they use is the one and only Stacey Michel. She looks nice, but she's a right, nasty bitch."

"That sounds like the right bunch."

"I'll send you their photos plus some background info but be careful. They're not only tough bastards but clever, especially the boss, Barry Whitehead."

"Okay Sugar, thanks. If I hear any rumours regarding weapons and drugs, I'll let you know."

George said, "So what the hell is their motive? Why go to all the trouble to get the dirt on our barrister friend and not do anything with it?"

"George, the barrister defends people for a living. Maybe they have a mate who's due for trial and they'll hire her to win by fair means or foul."

"That makes sense. Get her blackmailed and then wait for the case to come up, yeah, I bet you're right, En."

"Yeah, but all we can do is wait; we just need a slice of luck."

The phone rang. Viv said, "Eneko, are you in, Jazz and Tank want to pop in?"

"Yeah, of course. We'll put the coffee on."

Tank and Jasmin arrived, Jasmin straight off a night shift. She looked tired. "

I said, "Thank God, Tank's with you. That means I can keep my clothes on."

Jasmin looked at me. "Next week will be fine. But Tank and I have some other news. It's delicate. You know I run a group for people with addictions or dependency problems, well one of my patients, who is a heroin user, but you'd never know it, is a physical wreck right now and I thought it was just a drug problem but it's more. He was almost beside himself, shaking and frightened. It's doctor patient confidentiality, and I shouldn't be saying this."

Tank interrupted, "The bloke was the van driver on the wages robbery."

"Wow!" said George. "So where do we go with this bit of information? Blackmail is becoming very popular. The poor bloke — that's the real shitty end of the stick."

"Tank?"

"Eneko, the guy is a mess, worried about his job, his wife, and his kids. Only his wife knows about his addiction, another poor bloke who got addicted during the war. The blackmail was all done over the phone, along with threats of beating up his wife. He couldn't figure out how they knew about his habit, but during the robbery, he noticed one bloke had a webbed finger and he remembers noticing a bloke like that when he was getting some drugs. He reckoned it was months ago, but it stuck in his mind."

"Brilliant, now we're getting somewhere. Tank, can you and Binns have a recce and see what turns up? And Jasmin, thanks, but we won't break any confidence you have with your patients."

Jasmin smiled. "I know, but won't it be like a needle in a haystack?"

"Maybe, but people get nicknames. The names stick, so we may get lucky, and I'll try Sugar. He may have heard something. Okay, let's get to it and we'll catch up tomorrow sometime."

Tank and Jasmin left, and a young bloke entered. "Excuse me, are you Eneko?"

"That's me."

"I'm Sammy. I work for Binns, and he's asked me to come and pick up your car keys so I can move it out of the way while we're working at the cooperage."

I threw Sammy the car keys, "Thanks mate."

He smiled. "I like the decor here."

George said, "You've got taste Sammy. I'm George, by the way."

"Hi George, I'll see you later."

When Sammy had gone, Viv laughed, "What a heartbreaker you are, George. You've got all the young men eating out of your hand. Little Eric won't like the competition."

George stuck her tongue out at us and said, "More coffee?"

"Yep," I said as I picked up the phone. I dialled the police station.

"Hi, it's Eneko Sora. Is Inspector Shaw available, please? Okay, that's fine, thanks again. Sugar's secretary will get him to call us later."

"George, coffee time at the Kardomah, I'm buying."

George grabbed her jacket and so did I. The sky looked hopeful and there was still some warmth in the air.

"I wonder when dear Stacey is going to get in touch with our barrister."

George replied, "I think it might be the secretary Stacey gets in touch with first. She thinks she's the easier option, but I don't."

"It's an interesting one. I think we're going to nip it in the bud before it ever gets near to going to court. We can do that. The police can't."

"So, how do we do that?"

"We teach them a lesson they'll never forget."

"You mean go in all guns blazing?"

"Yeah, I mean all masked up and shoot them if we have to. Otherwise, a good lumping, in the words of Inspector Sugar."

"I love it when you talk tough. It makes me want to kiss you."

"I can talk like this all day, George."

"Oh! You know how to give a girl a good time."

I laughed, George giggled, and we got a big smile from Ruby as we trooped in.

"The usual, Ruby, please," said George.

"You two are all smiles this morning. Anything you want to tell me?"

"Well," said George, "Where should I start: En knows how to give a girl a good time, or so the fiery one he was with last night told me, he's not just a pretty face."

"Tell me more, George, but only when En's not here, don't want to make him blush."

George winked and said, "I can't say anymore, Ruby. It's all very hush-hush."

I raised my eyebrows. George laughed. Ruby waved the phone receiver and George went over. She had a quick conversation and came back. She opened her purse, took out a notebook and wrote the name Joe Briggs—webbed finger and Garston boys.

"So, Sugar came up trumps. Can you give Binns a ring, George, and see if he knows the name, or has heard of the Garston boys?"

George went over and made a couple of calls. There was lots of nodding and then she looked at her watch and said, okay. My lip-reading skills were improving.

"En, no joy with Joe Briggs, but Tank has heard of the Garston boys. He's on his way over, should be 15 minutes."

George ordered some more coffees, and we waited. George was nattering to Ruby, and I was trying to plan something that hadn't happened yet! A bit of a waste of time! Tank arrived and Ruby came round the bar and kissed him on the cheek. He smiled, and she kissed him again. George and Tank came over and Ruby brought over the coffees.

"Morning, Eneko. I've made a couple of calls, and the Garston boys are the ones you're after. I know they hang out on the Cassy, a couple of Teds and fast cars but no real heavy hitters, but Binns is just checking with a mate about this Joe Briggs. He said he'd ring here if he finds out anything."

"Things are moving, En."

The phone rang again, and Ruby waved. Tank got up and answered it. He had a quick conversation and came back to the table.

"Binns said this Joe Briggs character hangs out with the Brownlow Hill mob, a real nasty piece of work, wartime spivs who still think the war is on, they need taking care of."

"Tank, you and Binns are in form. That's great work. How do you see it panning out?"

"Me and Binns will do a recce, but I'm worried about the van driver. He's terrified and so is his wife. She thinks they're ruined."

"No, he won't. I'll square it with Sugar. We'll say he was working with us and the police on an inside job, and we couldn't tell the port authorities in case it got leaked. Sugar will love that; it makes the force look like they have irons in the fire all over the place."

"Jesus Eneko, that would be a result. I'm off to get Binns, will call you or George later."

"En, you've got your head working all right, now if only the barrister's case would be that easy?"

We finished up our coffees and George said she'd go back to the office. I tried to catch Begonia at her office, but the secretary said she was in her art class, so I walked over to the college. The receptionist said he was in Studio 3 on the second floor. I peeped through the window and saw Begonia and Zoriona sitting back-to-back, naked and being sketched by a small group of artists. Zoriona caught my eye, and I nodded and left. I wandered back to the office and made a call to Sugar; he was in and said he'd see me in the White Star in ten minutes. Viv was busy typing, so I made her a cup of coffee. She smiled.

George arrived, I said, "You and I have a date with Sugar in the White Star in five minutes."

"Right, give me two minutes."

She said to Viv, "Can you call this number and tell the secretary who you are and fix an appointment for her to meet me somewhere tomorrow?"

"Okay George, see you later. And Eneko, say hi to the tall man with big shoes from me."

"Oh, I get it tall man, big shoes, and you call me! Mind you, his other nickname at school was ten pence."

They both looked at me, mystified, and then George said, "You mean?"

Viv laughed and said, "That long! Jesus!"

George said, "That's what his wife says every time he gets into bed."

"Oh, get Begonia sketching him. I'll sit with him and just look..."

"See you later, Viv."

"Yes, boss, and thank you for that thought. But you are a growing boy, you know."

"I might mention this to Binns, you know!"

"Good, it'll give him something to aspire to."

On the way to the White Star, George was chuckling away to herself, "Our Viv's true self is coming out, eh! Just shows you what working with me does to the staff."

Before I could add anything, Sugar came round the corner. George kissed him on the cheek and complimented him on his new black brogue shoes, "What size are they then, Sugar?"

"Size 14. They are a bugger to find."

I gave George a look.

Sugar said, "So what's up? It sounded urgent."

"It is, but let's get a drink first." Maggie was on duty, George waved us into the backroom, and she ordered the drinks. Sugar looked up. George started, "The wages robbery we now know who was involved, a gang called the Garston boys and our webbed-hand friend, Joe Briggs, who hangs out with the Brownlow Hill boys. But it's complicated, Sugar, so bear with me and don't get mad, okay?"

George outlined the whole thing: the distraught wife, the van driver, his addiction, and fears of losing his job.

I then outlined the plan of saying that he was working undercover for us and the police.

Sugar looked calm. "I can live with that. No sense in putting a load of grief on hard-working folk, but how do we apprehend them?"

George said, "Binns and Tank are working on it now. We hope to have a line on them soon."

"Okay, but keep me up to date. It'll take me a couple of hours to get the lads lined up and ready for action. Any weapons likely to be involved, Eneko?"

"Tank reckons they're stupid enough to have some."

"Okay you two, I'll leave you to it but do nothing stupid and leave the arrests to us and don't worry, I'll sort out the van driver's problem."

Sugar departed; Maggie gave him her best smile. George said, "I do like a new pair of brogue shoes."

I shook my head. "Let's get back to the office and see if anything has happened."

Viv was typing away, "George, Binns just phoned, could you go over to Frank's? They want you to check on the kitchen. Here's the drawing Binns made."

"Okay, I'll nip over and see my new admirer, young Sammy."

"Any news on Frank? Viv?"

"Yes, Jazz just rang. They're pleased with him. He's laughing and joking and eating well, just itching to get back home."

"Brilliant. Hope he'll like his new place."

"Fancy a coffee, boss. I'm just going to put one on before the kids arrive."

"Yeah, thanks, Viv. How are the kids taking the news about Frank?"

"I guess they think he'll be back just the same, but young Eric loves him to bits, so he'll be alright."

George came back in. "They are doing a fantastic job over there, the bathroom is already done, and the kitchen looks fab. I might move in with Frank. Sammy gave me your keys, En. Viv, you missed lunch, so when the kids get here you take off and we'll see you in the morning."

The door flew open and in came the twins. "Mum, we're starving."

"Now there's a surprise, so grab my bag, Eric, and we'll be off."

"See you George, see you Eneko. Can I clean your car this weekend?"

I laughed, "You can indeed, young man."

Chapter 11—Zoriona gets in the bath

Peace reigned! George shut the office. "I'll put the bath on, but first, let's do some work and maybe some target practice. I think we're going to need it."

I thought George was right. The workout went well. We worked on some technical moves around kicking low and very hard. We then did some squats with heavy weights; George did that effortlessly. Practice with the pistols went well. We both hit our targets. We went back upstairs, and Begonia and Zoriona were waiting outside. George opened the door.

Begonia said, "Zoriona is fascinated by the Japanese bath. And we saw you this afternoon, Eneko peeping into our live class. George, we were posing for an all-ladies' class. I think we frightened Eneko off. Anyway, we're here to try the bath and don't worry Eneko, Zoriona is a naturist of many years standing as is her mother. So, we're just going to get some towels from the flat. See you in the bath."

George laughed, "Another young, nubile body for you to look at. It's a hard life, eh, En? The wrong word to use there." We got undressed, washed, and got into the bath with care as the water was red hot. Zoriona and Begonia came in, took off their dressing gowns, and Begonia showed Zoriona what to do before getting in the bath. As Zoriona got in, she gasped, "It's red hot."

George said, "The best thing is to slide in and don't move, then it doesn't burn as much."

Begonia started talking, "An excellent class today, only women, but from all walks of life, everyone from sales ladies to barristers, but a fantastic group, weren't they Zoriona?"

Zoriona nodded, not moving a muscle.

George said, "The barrister wasn't a tall, slim lady with red hair?"

"How did you know George? Are you playing detective again?"

I'd caught on, "When's the next class, Begonia?"

"Friday, we do classes for the ladies on Tuesdays and Fridays."

"Excellent, I've got a new person to sit next time, a muscular specimen, and an excellent body to sketch."

"Who?"

"Why George, of course, she was just telling me today she'd love to try it."

"George, you never mentioned it before?"

George smiled at me and said, "Yeah, why not? It sounds fun. Maybe Zoriona and I could do it together?"

"Brilliant, I'll organise it for this Friday. Is that okay for you, too, Zoriona?"

Zoriona nodded. I said, "Zoriona, that's enough for your first time, otherwise you'll be sweating all night."

Zoriona climbed out of the bath, she was like a beetroot, George climbed out too, "Zoriona I've got some moisturising cream that'll take the sting out of it."

The girls left me at peace. I took about ten minutes and then climbed out. The girls were all sitting down on the sofas drinking white wine.

"Eneko, that was the most marvellous bath I've ever had. Will you invite me again?"

"Zoriona, you don't need to ask. We're here most evenings."

"Oh! Thank you, I feel so clean!"

"Maybe George could organise a lady's night and get Viv as well. Ah! Begonia, how's the sketch of the ladies going? I'm dying to have a look at it?"

"Give me until next week. Oh! I forgot to tell you; the college has asked me to exhibit them. They've let me have a small studio and I'm going to exhibit about 10 sketches."

"That's great news. Just need more clients for you," said Zoriona.

"I've got more. Ruby wants me to sketch her, warts and all she said, she'd love to sit naked for me!"

The girls said they were going to get changed in their flat and I said I'd walk Zoriona back to her place. She said living with Jasmin and Tank was lovely, but she wanted to get a place on her own. I said I'd keep an eye out for anything suitable. She kissed me on the cheek and said goodnight.

I was up with the lark, but George beat me to it. I heard the office door open. She shouted, "Are you decent, En?"

I muttered, "Yes." And threw on my gym gear and we went down to the gym. The session woke me up alright and after a quick shower I headed into the office, where the smell of toast and coffee was enticing.

"Morning boss, coffee, and toast are ready."

"Thanks Viv."

"George is just over at Frank's place again. Her young admirer, Sammy, came calling."

George came in. "The coffee smells good."

Viv said, "They are tearing the upper floor to bits at Frank's place. It looks like a major overhaul. There must be five or six tradesmen over there."

"Yeah, young Sammy showed me around. They're doing an excellent job. It'll look brilliant when they've finished."

"En, take a seat. We need to go over this plan about the barrister. What is it you want me to say to her?"

"Well, I thought you could go for a drink and get the latest information. I'll book you a room at the Adelphi. You know for God and company and see how it goes. I mean, she will have seen you naked. I don't think you'd have to say very much."

George shook her head, "En, there are times, but if push comes to shove, you never know," and grinned.

She leant over and whispered in my ear, "Don't mention Frank's place, okay. Binns is making an apartment on the top floor for Viv and the kids so they can be near Frank, and then he's going to sort out Viv's place for Zoriona, if that's okay with you?"

"You're getting too clever by halves, partner. I think that's a wonderful idea, nice one, Binns."

The phone rang. Viv picked it up, "Yes he is, I'll put him on."

Chapter 12—Geoff gets in touch

Viv handed me the receiver and mouthed, "Geoff."

"Morning Geoff, how's things?" Geoff gave me the information we'd been waiting to hear. A long conversation followed, with Geoff signing off by saying, "You didn't hear this from me, okay?"

I handed the phone back to Viv; George raised her eyebrows.

"We're in business. Geoff said he was going into a gambling den when he almost bumped into an old school friend who was leaving and looked the worse for wear. Geoff said nothing. Inside, he chatted to one dealer, who was on a break, and he mentioned that Geoff's old mate was way over his head in debt. Geoff didn't give it much thought until he woke up this morning and then he realised the old school friend is now a custom's officer."

"We need to talk to Sugar, En. This could be the break he's looking for.

"I'll get him on the phone right now."

For a change, Sugar answered, "Eneko here, mate. We've come up with someone, a customs officer called Roger Stafford, who appears to have enormous gambling debts with the wrong people."

Sugar said, "Good man, it smells right. Just need to find out which docks he works at and what rota. Leave it with me and I'll get back to you."

"George, we need to come up with a battle plan. We need info and photos on the Garston boys. Binns and Tank are on that. We need to get the info on the barrister, the secretary, and Stacey Michel and crew."

"En, okay, the barrister is called Eres. The secretary is Ceri. I'll get photos on Friday at the life class. The Garston gang is what Binns and Tank are checking right now. We need them to get one of Joe Briggs and the customs officer, Roger Stafford."

The phone rang. Viv picked it up, "Yes, she is, just a moment, please. Viv mouthed, barrister."

"Hi, George speaking, that's novel. When is this going to happen? Okay, I'll see you at the life class on Friday. Yeah, I'm the sitter. Yes, it is an unusual way to get introduced! See you on Friday, or rather you'll see me on Friday."

I looked at George.

"Stacey Michel just phoned her. She wants to see her and Ceri on the Woodside Ferry tomorrow at noon, instructions to be given later. But it gives you the opportunity to snap everyone and see which gang members are looking on."

"Good, and then on Friday after the life class, you can get all the details from Eres. I'll get my cameras loaded and then I'm ready to go."

Viv looked over. "This is getting exciting. Can I do anything to help?"

George smiled, "You are Vee. Don't be daft. You're in charge of the info coming through the office."

Viv beamed, "Yeah, I guess so."

The phone rang again. Viv picked up, "Hi Tank, oh good I'll tell the boss right now, when are you due back, 3 pm, okay see you later."

"Boss, they've got all the photos. Binns will drop them off later for you to develop."

"Thanks, Viv. George, we need to find out which ships are coming into port that look dodgy. You know, an irregular route or something. I wonder if Begonia would know. That could be a job for our in-house investigative journalist, Zoriona, maybe?"

"En, that could be difficult. Zee's only been in the country for five minutes, but with Bee's help, you never know. I'll meet up with them for lunch at the Kardomah."

"Right, George, I'll give Sugar another call and see if he knows anything."

I rang Sugar. He was struggling with the same problem. We discussed various ideas, ports of departure, which country was more probable, and what ships. The more we talked, the more we got confused. The only lead Sugar had was Roger Stafford, who was going to be on duty at Canada dock and Brunswick dock for the next week or so.

Maybe the girls could come up with a more profitable line of enquiry.

The phone rang, Viv answered, "She mouthed, Lavina," I nodded, "Yes, he's in" and passed me the phone.

"Morning Lavina, yes, all good, thanks. Ah! A new range of wool suits and overcoats for winter. Of course I'm interested, aren't I your best customer? I tell you what, I've got a couple of hours free. I'll nip over now, and you can buy me coffee."

Viv laughed, "Boss, you're a real dandy at heart. Can't wait to see the new you!"

I bowed, George laughed, "We need some more cases just to pay for your clothes."

We left the office together; I headed up towards the Pier Head and George cut through to the Kardomah. I arrived at Watson and Prickard and spotted Lavina. She waved and took me through to the men's department. The sales assistant looked up, smiled, and went back to his work. Lavina picked out some suits for me to try on. They fitted well. She also got shirts and accessories to match. Then we came to overcoats, some of them very heavyweight, but she found me a lovely lightweight Merino wool Italian coat which looked the business. So I now had a new winter wardrobe. Lavina caught my arm and took me to the ladies' underwear department. I bought some in George's size in black. Lavina laughed. And then I bought a scarf for Viv. I paid. Lavina kissed me on the cheek, and I left in a very good mood.

On the way back to the office, I almost went to the Kardomah to catch up with the girls, but on second thoughts I left them to come up with the ideas. And anyway, Binns would be back soon with the photos. I was just passing the White Star when Tank stuck his head out and waved me in.

"Eneko, I've got the photos. Binns has gone over to the job at Frank's place, and I've got some news. Not good."

Maisy held up a glass and a bottle of mineral water. I nodded.

"So, what's the news, Tank?"

"We found out where the Garston gang hang out, no problem. Binns got plenty of photographs. Then we went up to Brownlow Hill and got a couple of photos of a certain Joe Briggs. He was in his local, but he was chatting to Viv's ex! I thought Binns was going to go mental, but he didn't. But what are we going to do?"

"We find the money. Get as much evidence as possible and then sort the lot of them out for good, especially that ex of Viv's. That piece of scum is mine. But say nothing to Viv. You, me, and George need to have a conversation about this."

"Okay, Eneko. Binns said he'll see you back at the office."

"Right, Tank, do me a favour and nip up to the Kardomah. George is with Zoriona and Begonia, and on your way back to the office, bring George up to speed."

"I'm on it."

Binns was just coming across from Frank's place as I turned up the lane.

"Eneko, I've got the photos. You'll never guess who it was..."

"I've just seen Tank, he's brought me up to date, don't you go off on one, he's mine, employer's rights, okay?"

"Whatever you say, Eneko. But we need to get ready for all eventualities, mate."

"I know, but go on, give me some good news. How's the new apartment coming along?"

"It's looking good. Frank's ground-floor flat is done, apart from the curtains, etc., and upstairs is about three quarters of the way there. And then when Viv and kids are in, I'll get the lads to start on redecorating your flat that Viv's been living in."

"I'm loving this mate, but remember, I'm paying for the work done on my property and when you finish, I'd like you to start on George and Begonia's place. And I'm not taking no for an answer."

Binns laughed, "I know a determined face when I see one, okay, mate?"

We went into the office; I left Viv and Binns to it and took the film downstairs to get developed. I was just about to start when there was a knock on the door. "En, it's me. Can I come in?"

I opened the door. "What's up?"

"Nothing, En. I'd just like to learn how to develop film. Is that okay?"

"Sure, just watch and if you have questions, just ask?" I went through the process stage by stage. George picked it up, so she developed the last film. We then went through the printing process and left the films to dry.

"Eneko, I have had a chat with Bee and Zee about the docks our customs officer has been assigned to. The girls said it should make it be simpler. Zee is going to look at routes and where the drugs originate. Zee is up for it."

"Good, then tomorrow we need to be on the ball regarding Stacey Michel. We'll have a chat with Binns and Tank about them trailing the wonderful Miss Michel and her mates tomorrow as they get off the Woodside ferry."

In the office, Binns, Tank, George, and I worked out a plan of action for tomorrow. The idea being to follow them and find out their HQ.

"And then what, Eneko? " asked Tank.

"Then we do a number on them and make them never want to set foot in this city again."

"Then it could get messy," said Binns.

There was a knock at the door. Viv answered and said, "Bring them in, please. It's your shopping, boss."

I thanked the courier and carried the bags to my apartment. I heard Viv say, "Binns, you should take a leaf out of Eneko's books and spend some money on clobber that wasn't around during the war." I heard gales of laughter, then the twins arrived, and George said, "Right, you two help mum with her bags and you, young Eric, I want that book finished off tonight, questions tomorrow after school."

Binns and Tank left with them.

George said, "Let's look at our photos. Maybe we should get some across to Sugar?"

We went down to the gym, the photos looked good, I didn't recognise anyone except Viv's ex and Joe Briggs, who looked older and a lot meaner.

George put the bath on, and I said I would join her. She said, "Bee and Vee were going to work late and try to come up with some answers to our shipping problem."

I put the photos in one envelope for us, some in an envelope for Sugar. George called a taxi, and the driver was there with inside a couple of minutes. George handed the envelope over with instructions. The driver waved.

"En, I'm going to get in the bath."

I went into my place and got the parcel of George's new underwear. I left it outside on the sofa and went into the bathroom. The bath felt great. We were both lost in our own thoughts. George decided she'd had enough and climbed out of the bath and went into the apartment.

I called out, "George, the parcel on the sofa is for you." I didn't hear a word, but when I went out. George was dressed in her new black underwear. She looked sensational.

She kissed me on the cheek, "En, they are lovely, thank you. Any reason?"

"I just want you to look good before you take your clothes off at the life class on Friday."

"We get naked before the class begins, En."

"Ah, of course. But beautiful underwear always gets noticed."

"En, what are you like, so now chop chop, I want to see what you bought for yourself, starting with your underwear."

I tried on my new clothes; George loved my new suits and my overcoat. She was sure I'd make an impression anywhere, but even more so with black brogue shoes. I smiled, almost.

"En, I'm off to my place. I'll catch up with the girls and see if they've found anything."

"Okay, see you in the morning."

I poured myself a Remy and got my notebook and wrote the ideas we'd come up with in the last couple of days. The Garston boys were a problem. We needed to find the cash and then let Sugar take over. The Brownlow Hill gang. We could leave for now, but Joe Briggs and Viv's ex needed to be taught a proper lesson. Tomorrow we would see what Stacey Michel had up her sleeve, and then she and her gang needed to be put out of operation. We were going to be busy.

The morning broke, the rain was pouring down, and the thermometer had dropped. I was working out when George joined me. We did about an hour and then went and got showered. The office was busy when I arrived. Sugar was talking to Viv and drinking coffee.

"Morning Eneko, I'm drinking your coffee and chatting up your secretary."

"Morning boss, this police officer demanded coffee and toast, and said he knew you."

"Disgraceful, I'll have to set my business partner on him, Morning George. You're just in time to evict this man masquerading as a police officer."

"Eneko, looking at the size of those feet, I'm pretty sure he's a rozzer."

Sugar laughed, "It's an act, you two have got going there. I've called round to have a chat about the Garston boys. Those photos you sent over rang a few bells with one of my constables. I've written it down, and it's on Viv's desk. But what I want to talk about is shipping. And our customs officer. I assume you got the info from your Chinese mate. Don't look surprised, Eneko. I'm not just a pretty face."

I said, "Well, now we don't know a lot. George has been investigating, along with Begonia, about ships and cargos, but it's like looking for a needle in a haystack. However, we know his work schedule so we might have a chance.

The phone rang, George took it, "Hi Bee, what's up?" George's conversation didn't last long. "Okay, see you later."

"Bee reckons it could be one of two ships docking tonight, but she said she put her money on one called the SS Breton, which was loaded at Hong Kong, then Saigon which she said is unusual then India, and two ports in West Africa before coming to the UK. She also said in India they picked up a large amount of canned fruit, which is packed in syrup and destined for a company in Liverpool, based in Kirkdale."

"Which dock is it, George?"

"Canada dock, Sugar. So it's pretty close to Kirkdale."

"Can I use the phone, Viv, please?"

He dialled, "It's Shaw here. Where is our customs officer due to be tonight? Okay, gotcha, I'll be back in an hour."

He looked at me, "I think Begonia is right, our customs officer is going to be on duty this evening at Canada dock. So, we'll be there, watching. Say thanks to Begonia, I'm off. I'll give you a buzz in the morning and let you know what happened."

Chapter 13—Man with camera

"Right George, I'm going to get my camera ready. Do you want to come along?"

"I'll spot the two of them for you. Do I wear a disguise, En?"

"Well, as it's pouring with rain, I think an umbrella and a mac should do it. In fact, the umbrella is perfect. I can take the photos from under it without being seen. But let's go early and park. Then, if they have a car, we can follow them."

George went to get the Land Rover from Frank's place, and I got my mac with the big pockets, which were large enough for my camera and lenses. George tooted the horn. I waved goodbye to Viv and joined George in the car. George drove down to the Pier Head and parked up just past the tram stop. We did a recce, with George holding the umbrella, it made it easy for me to take photos. After a few practice shots of passengers on the ferry, I felt good to go. Not ideal, but it would suffice on the ferry. We'd have to take a chance that they wouldn't spot us.

"En, why don't we go over to Woodside and come back on the ferry so we're already on it? Then we can see if anybody is shadowing Stacey Michel?"

"Sounds like a plan. Let's do it."

We boarded the ferry and remained inside; the rain battered against the portholes. The tide was on the turn, the ferry started rolling, and the wind was blowing the spray all over the upper deck. Few passengers rode between rush hours. George had her hair tied up under a woollen hat and with the umbrella up, no one would recognise her. We got off the ferry at Woodside and had a walk around for about half an hour, then we headed back for the ferry that Stacey said she was going to be on. We boarded the ferry and went to the upper deck. George put the umbrella up and we cuddled together like a courting couple.

As we reached the Pier Head and the passengers boarded, George whispered, "Eres is the tall redhead in the black overcoat. Ceri is the shorter woman in the green duffle coat."

They came up onto the upper deck, even with the rain. George and I moved towards the stern, still acting like a courting couple. I started getting my camera ready. George nudged me and turned so I could see better. A very good-looking lady dressed in navy blue walked up to Eres and Ceri and kissed them both on the cheek and started talking. I took a few photos; George was shielding me very well. The conversation lasted until we reached Woodside, where Eres and Ceri got off. Stacey stayed onboard but went down to stand in the dry. George and I stayed out in the open and waited. We disembarked at the Pier Head and still huddled together under the umbrella; we followed Stacey at a discreet distance. She looked like she was heading for the Overhead Railway but walked past the staircase and stood at the curb on the Strand. We walked past and headed for our car. George got in the driving seat, and I looked back towards Stacey Michel. A black Jaguar stopped, and she got in. We let it go past and then we followed.

"Give them plenty of room, George. It's an easy car to follow."

George nodded and let the Jag go. We travelled along the docks all the way to the Dingle, where the Jag stopped and waited. The Overhead must have arrived because quite a few passengers started coming up from the station. Two blokes got in the car and then it drove off again.

George said, "Those two were on the ferry. They must have been tracking Stacey Michel. Do you think they spotted us?"

"I doubt it. We must have looked like a courting couple."

The Jag went down through Aigburth and along towards Garston before turning up to Mossley Hill and stopping at a large, detached house. George drove past and parked. The rain was drumming down, but the sky was brightening. We waited for about twenty minutes; the rain had almost stopped. I got out and went around to the side of the house. I saw a wall and thought that if I climbed it, they would see me.

I joined George and said, "Let's find a telephone box." George spied one next to Mossley Hill station. I rang the office. Viv answered.

"Viv is Binns about?"

"I'll put him on, boss."

"What's up Eneko?"

"I've got a job for you and Tank tonight. We've followed this blackmailing gang to a house in Mossley Hill. I'd like you to drop in and do what you do and get us some answers, but it may take a while, as they've only just got back."

"Okay Eneko. I'll get all the info off you later. In the meantime, I'll get Tank primed and ready."

"Okay, see you soon."

"George, let's get back to the office."

At the office, Tank and Binns were ready, and I explained our plan. Binns nodded, and he and Tank took off. Viv had already left with the twins and Begonia phoned to say she was working on the sketch with Zoriona and would be round a bit later, for a bath maybe? George went down to the gym to check that the weapons were all loaded and ready. I was still trying to work out how we could get the upper hand with Stacey and the gang when the phone rang. Tank was ringing from Mossley Hill Station. He'd just spotted Stacey arrive in a car and drag a woman into the house, a woman in a green duffle coat!

"Okay, Tank, George and I are on our way. Where are you parked, okay got it. See you in 20 minutes?"

I ran down to the gym, George, "Grab the guns. They've got Ceri at the house in Mossley Hill."

"Okay, I've got the guns, En. You grab the Land Rover and let's get moving."

We raced over to Mossley Hill, spotted Binns's Land Rover and parked just up the road from them. The rain had left the roads flooded in places with huge puddles on the sides of the roads. No pedestrians would be out tonight. We waited until it went dark. Binns and Tank did a recce and came back after about 10 minutes.

"Stacey has got that woman tied up in a back room. The woman looks terrified. The three blokes are in another room, drinking and laughing. But there are two other heavies making something to eat in the kitchen."

"Okay, George, you take Stacey out and grab Ceri. Tank, you take out the two in the kitchen and Binns and I will sort out the laughing boys. Balaclavas on, no names. When we've got them, all subdued, Binns will go through the safe and get any photos, money, anything, and everything to destroy their racket. If they go for their guns, so be it. Okay, let's do it."

Binns opened the back door and pointed us to our target rooms. When we were at our respective doors, Binns yelled, "Go!"

And we crashed through doors. I went for Billy and Brian. They put up some resistance, but both went to the ground unconscious. Binns had got Barry the boss under control, so I raced into the kitchen to see the two heavies lying flat out on the kitchen floor. I nodded to Tank and went to see how George was faring. She had Stacey crumpled up on the sofa, moaning. Ceri was weeping, George untied her and motioned to her to stop weeping, or the gag would go back on.

So far, so good. We bound and gagged the lot and put them in the Jag and a big Ford parked at the side of the house. I went back inside, and Binns was already working on the safe. It was open within minutes. Tank smiled. He was impressed. Inside the safe were a load of brown files with names and photos inside, plus negatives, and a large amount of cash. Binns packed all this into a large canvas bag. I signalled to George, and we went looking for evidence of photo equipment and a developing room. We found it in the basement. Along with cameras and an array of weapons, but no guns.

I said to George, "Drop Ceri off at her home and give her this note, which tells her to take a few days off. She's got bruises all over her face, and not to mention tonight to anyone."

"Bit over the top, En?"

"No, we don't want anyone to know us. So, get going and I'll see you back at my place later."

Binns had got everything packed away. He and tank were waiting for me.

"What's the plan, Eneko?"

"I was going to suggest, we dump the cars outside the police station but on second thoughts, let's bring them back into the house, throw some evidence around, including some cash, the police will love that and then, even more so when they find all the photo gear and weapons in the basement."

"Sounds good, Eneko."

We put the villains back in the house. By now, some of them were conscious and threatening us with death threats. Binns made the phone call and when we left. We made sure all the doors and windows were open. As we left, the rain started hammering down again. We got back in Binn's Land Rover and drove back to the office.

Binns passed me the bag. "You check it, Eneko, and we'll see you in the morning." Tank gave me a big grin.

Chapter 14—A profitable night

George was in the office, Coffee was almost ready, the Remy on the table.

"Any problems, George?"

"No, Ceri was babbling. Stacey had given her a bit of a beating. She'd seen us on the ferry and wanted to know who we were and why we were doing this. I dropped her off. She was in quite a state, but I doubt if she'll remember much in the morning."

"Good, we left the others tied up with evidence all over the place for the police to find. I'm not sure what the police will charge them with, but whatever it is, I think their blackmailing ring is kaput. Are Zoriona and Begonia not coming around for a bath?"

"They've been and gone. I've just put the heater back on, though."

"Good, I'm in the mood for a cleansing bath. But first, let's see what's in the bag."

George cleared the desk, and we emptied the contents out. Lots of money, George whistled. Loads of papers regarding targets they had either hit or were going to hit. It made interesting reading. George started going through the photos.

"Jesus! En, do you recognise her?" I nodded. There were a lot of well-known people with all their peccadilloes on show to the world.

"What do we do with these, En? They could ruin many people?"

"I know, George. But I think we should keep them in the safe in the cellar. You never know when that knowledge could come in handy."

"Eneko Sora, you are a genuine piece of work. If only people knew this side of you, they'd be shocked. I'm shocked."

"George, you're not shocked at all. You know me, and you like that side of me, anyway. Let's count the money and divvy it out and then get clean!"

"You're going to keep the money as well!"

"We're going to keep the money. How the hell do we give it back?"

"Wow, you are..."

"Count it!"

We counted it, it totalled £29,500 and change. That came to £7,000 each. The rest would go into the bonus box. George put the money into four bundles and pushed them into the office safe. George undressed, washed, and got into the bath; I did the same. We relaxed and enjoyed the hot water.

"So, what happens tomorrow with the life class?"

"Nothing, just go ahead as normal and see what Eres has to say and just follow your head. You may not have to say anything. It could be all over the news by then. Just remember to wear your black underwear!"

"So, what should I do with my wealth?"

"Invest it. George, maybe some more land or a house, something solid for your old age."

"A barrage of abuse followed. I assumed it was abuse, as it was in Welsh."

I laughed, and we climbed out of the bath, said our goodnights, and went to our respective beds.

When I awoke, I could hear voices. The girls were all in the office. Begonia and Zoriona suggesting poses for George at the sitting later, as they couldn't make it. Viv laughed and said, "Excuse me, lady of considerable experience talking, you two bugger off and let me sort George out."

Begonia and Zoriona waved and said, "See you tonight. We're cooking!"

I waved and poured myself a coffee. Viv was explaining to George the art of posing without getting tired and stiff.

I said, "Why don't you go into the flat and practice? I'll look after the office."

"Brillant," said Viv and the girls disappeared into the flat.

The phone rang. I had a bet with myself concerning the identity of the caller. I won.

"Morning, Sugar, what can I do for you?"

"Well young Eneko, as you don't read newspapers, I'll just read you the headlines: Mossley Hill gang apprehended over blackmail charges."

"Well, that's a result for your boys."

"Not really, because they were all bound and gagged in their living room, quite amusing, but they're nicked."

"And again, the value of a certain Mr Shaw goes ever upward."

"Eneko, take care. Let's catch up next week for a pint or two?"

"Will do."

Binns and Tank walked in, "Morning Eneko?"

"Morning lads." I opened the safe and gave them their bundles of cash.

"£7,000 each, so don't go throwing it around on riotous living, save it for a rainy day."

Tank looked stunned; he couldn't get his words out.

Binns just laughed, "I love working with you, never a dull moment and always very well paid."

I said, "keep it quiet. Viv and George are in the apartment, so maybe get going and find a safe place for it."

They both raised their cash and said, "See you later."

George and Viv came out into the office. George looked nervous to me, although I knew she'd never admit it.

I said, "Viv, why don't you sit with George at lunch? I'll look after the office. It's only for a couple of hours."

"Are you sure, boss?"

"Yeah."

"Brilliant, we've just time for a quick shower. Must look our best, eh, George?"

I laughed. George smiled and mouthed, "Thank you."

The girls got ready and went on their way, "I said, break a leg, George."

I sat down with my notebook and tried to go through all the things we needed to do and put them in order of priority. The drug deal seemed to be in the hands of the law. We could only look on and keep a wary eye. This Brownlow Hill gang was bothering me, especially as Viv's ex was back on the scene. Maybe a word with Sugar could do the trick. I knew he'd be furious as the lad was told not to come back. Decisions, decisions.

The phone rang. I picked it up. "Sora speaking."

"Hi Eneko, it's Eddie, Frank's nephew. How are you?"

"Hi Eddie, all good, mate, and you?"

"Yeah good, thanks. I've just been in to see Frank and he was telling me about Binns doing up his flat. That's brilliant. I know he's looking forward to getting back home. But that's not the main reason for calling. Remember when we had that gang moving stuff around on the wagon? Well, I've just noticed on my duty roster for early tomorrow morning a late change of goods, canned fruit from India coming from a ship arriving in Brunswick dock tonight."

"Eddie, you are a bloody star. Can you keep track of it and see if it's loaded onto a train or a lorry?"

"Will do, Eneko. Take my phone number?"

"Thanks, Eddie." I wrote the number down in my notebook. Tomorrow morning, that would take a bit of planning. This drug gang sounded very organized, with dummy trails and ships. It must mean a big delivery. I called Binns and suggested we all get together this evening after Begonia and Zoriona had gone, say, around 10 pm. A phone call to Sugar but his secretary said he was out and about, but she would leave a message for him to ring me later this afternoon or this evening. Time to plan. Viv came in about 3 pm.

"How did it go?"

"George was fine. I think most of the ladies were sketching Miss Muscles. She looks bloody amazing. I think I'm going to train. Maybe George could give Bee, Zee, and me lessons. There was a tall-slim-redhead who was drooling. I think Bee's got competition! George is going to be swamped with admirers soon. I want those admiring glances at my rear end, from both men and women. I don't care."

I laughed, "Eddie rang. He's been in to see our patient and Frank is looking forward to getting home."

Viv said, "That's brilliant news. Have you seen the flat yet? It looks perfect and young Sammy has got excellent taste in fabrics and colours. He picked out all the curtains, rugs, and colours for the sofas and chairs. The other lads took the micky, but Binns told him he'd done a fantastic job and hired him full time! Sammy was so pleased."

I smiled, just as the twins came bursting through the door, "What's for tea, mum?"

"Come on, home for tea and then tomorrow we can see Uncle Frank in the hospital. I think he's going to come home next week."

"We better make sure that Frank's flat is ready then mum and there's enough tea and milk."

"Well, Helen, that's your job and Eric, you make sure you polish the brasses. Say goodbye to Eneko.

Chapter 15—A heart to heart with George

George returned about 5 pm. "I need a bath."

"It's already on. I thought you may need it."

"She gave me a look and went into the bathroom and stripped off.

"No underwear, I see."

George sighed, "For God and company. Eres kept my underwear as a memento. After the class, she asked me to go for a drink at her office. Her secretary was ill. She poured the drinks and started talking about the whole blackmail thing and Stacey Michel. She had to defend one of Stacey Michel's gang or she would face ruin. They were supposed to contact her today, but the news was all over the papers, and Eres was delighted. She knew it was us but said she'd never tell a soul and anyway, there was no proof. She was so thrilled; I thought she would faint. But she was so full of flattery that before I knew it, I was standing in her office naked. Talk about taking my knickers off. It was just like when I was sixteen, when I first met her. She seduced me, although I must admit I took little persuading. She complimented everything about me, my poise, physique, fashion sense. It was overwhelming. But I remembered I was the one in charge, so her arse is going to be very sore tomorrow after my bamboo cane did the business. So, if we ever need a barrister, I've got one eating out of my hand. But Eneko, if you ever tell anyone, I'll borrow Rhian's scissors."

I flinched, George laughed and kissed me on the cheek, "The things I do for you, Eneko."

"Well, Miss Popularity, I'll bring you up to date: Eddie has phoned, he reckons the drugs could be coming up to Edgehill, there's been a change of goods papers and Eddie thinks it looks dodgy. So, I think we'll cover the station tomorrow morning, and we'll leave the Canada dock job to Sugar. My view is that they've got a real load, so they're going to use both options, but I can't be sure, so we're going to be on our toes. Binns and Tank are coming round tonight at 10 pm for a meeting, so let's try to get the food and drink over by then. In fact, why don't we get out now and start the food operation off while Begonia and Zoriona get bathed?"

"I'm getting out now. Get some clothes on, En and I'll nip back and get some bloody underwear!"

I was getting changed when I heard the girls arrive. "Is there room in the bath for us?" shouted Begonia. George yelled something, and all I heard was laughter.

I went out into the kitchen, Begonia said, "Hi Eneko, we're just going to get a quick bath and get cooking. George has forgotten her underwear and is going up to the flat. She's getting worse."

I started cutting bread, uncorking some bottles of wine, and laying the table. George was back straight away in a knee length red skirt and a black roll-neck sweater. She looked lovely. She gave me a twirl, flipped her skirt to reveal no underwear, gave me a wink, and put her finger to her lips.

I just laughed.

The meal was very Basque, which went down well. George and I took it easy on the wine, as we had an early start the next morning.

Zoriona said, "I've written a story on Begonia, 'The Basque artist' in Liverpool. I think it will appear in the Echo soon and I've sent it to Bilbao with promises of photographs and a follow up when the exhibition goes ahead."

"Oh! That's brilliant, Zee."

"Yes, it's going to be an exhibition about feminism in the workplace, so I'm going to do some more sketches of women at work, Eneko gave me a superb idea about washerwomen and now I'm looking to work with female workers in breweries, tobacco factories, chimney sweeps and even lady bus drivers. I'm over the moon. Pedro has said

Zoriona, and I can work part time so we can concentrate more on our other jobs."

"What a shame. You won't need my sketch now for the exhibition."

"Don't worry En, they'll make an exception for you and your oh, so cute derriere!"

I decided that silence was my only defence. The girls thought it deserved much laughter. I went to whip George's skirt up, but she caught on and made a scissor sign with her right hand. We started clearing things away for the meeting. With kisses for us both, Begonia and Zoriona left. George pretended to lift her skirt, and I went and grabbed the bamboo cane. She said, "Pax partner." And went into the flat for some underwear.

Chapter 16—A bang in the night

The lads arrived, and we got down to planning. Binns said, "Looks like more rain tonight, so that should help us, but I think the only thing we can do is trail them and see where they end up and then inform Sugar. Otherwise, if they're armed, we're going to end up with a major firefight in the goods yard."

We all nodded our agreement and made 5 am as the time to meet. Unless Eddie rang me earlier. When they had left, I went down to the cellar and checked the weapons. I lay awake and at around 4 am, I heard the office door open and then water running. As I dressed, the aroma of coffee came wafting into my bedroom. I went into the office, George said, "Morning." And handed me a coffee and a cigarette. She had dressed all in black with her black duffle coat lying on the sofa. I handed her the gun, she checked it and put it in her duffle coat pocket. I sipped my coffee.

"En, Binns, and Tank are going up to Edgehill in their Land Rover. We'll go in yours. I'll drive."

"Okay, I'll take my camera. I know Binns has his, but we may get separated, and photos could be crucial."

"Do we suspect Joe Briggs and Viv's ex are involved in this?"

"George, I think so. There seem to be many people involved in this escapade, too many for my liking."

We left the office and got into the Land Rover and motored up to Edgehill. I'd phoned ahead to Eddie, so we didn't have any problems getting in. I could see Binns and Tank parked up by the signal box. As I got out of the Land Rover, it began to rain.

Binns walked over. "En, it looks like they are about to unload a freight car. They're waiting for a lorry by the look of things."

We waited and then we saw the lorry parked next to the freight car. Binns and I moved closer and took some photos. It would not be easy as the thunder reared its noisy head. I got as close as I could, then a flash of lightning caught me out in the open.

Viv's ex was looking right at me. He shouted, "Look out, it's the scuffers," and pulled a gun and started firing at me. I dived behind a freight car and George fired a couple of shots at Viv's ex. Next thing bullets were flying all over the place, I grabbed George, and we ran back along the tracks. I could just see Binns and Tank had the same idea, but the shooting didn't cease.

Tank ran over. "What the hell are they shooting at?"

Before I could reply, a tremendous explosion shook the freight yard and debris started flying and raining down on us. We took refuge under a freight car, then boom, another explosion. We stayed where we were. Then silence.

Binns said, "You lot beat it. I'll see what's happening with Eddie. See you for breakfast."

Tank and I jumped into the Land Rover, and George steered us out of the gate before any police or railway officials were on the scene. George drove, Tank whistled, "That was some bang, there were munitions amongst that and petrol. I have heard nothing that loud since South Korea."

"Jesus! No one would have survived that. We were so lucky.

George said, "En, was that Vee's ex who shot at you?"

"I'm sure it was, George. Must have been off his head shooting like that. Then it looked like his mates stared shooting at him and each other. Bloody bunch of nutters."

"Bloody bunch of dead nutters, Eneko. I hope Eddie and his mates are okay. They should be. The signal box is a fair distance away from that siding."

We reached the office. Luckily, we were too early for Viv, but she would be in soon. George put on the coffee and poured the Remy. We sat in silence, more in shock than anything else. The door opened and Binns walked in. "Eddie and his mates are okay, thank God! I had a quick shufty. The place is a mess. Thank God! It wasn't in a major part of the marshalling yard. So, it didn't do much damage to locomotive engines, but the area where they were unloading was just a hole in the ground. They'll be quite a few dead and there are bits of weapons and stuff all over place. No bugger lived through that."

George said, "What do we say to Viv, and do we tell Sugar?"

"There's nothing to say now. We'll see what the day brings, and then I'll talk to Sugar. Once we know more, we can speak to Viv.

The door opened and in walked Begonia, Jasmin, Zoriona, and Viv. Begonia said, "Did you hear that bang? It almost threw me out of bed. Is everybody okay?"

"Yeah, Bee, it was an explosion at the marshalling yards at Edgehill Station. It sounded bad, and I don't know if there were any injuries yet?"

Jasmin said, "There must be. They just ordered me to go to the hospital. Tank, can you give me a lift?"

George threw Tank the Land Rover keys, "See you later, Jazz."

I took the plunge. "Viv, I think your ex might have been involved. We saw him there just before the blast. Nobody could survive that."

Viv looked at me, came over and kissed me on the cheek, "Thanks for telling me straight, boss. He made his choice. I stopped worrying about him years ago. And to be honest, the kids don't even remember him.

"Vee, if you want some time off...?

"No George, I'd rather be busy. Come on Binns, help me get the little ones to school, then I can get back to work."

Begonia and Zoriona looked shocked. George grabbed them both, kissed them, sat them down and said, "Coffee En, please."

Silence reigned for about 10 minutes, then Begonia said, "Zoriona, do you fancy sitting today? I feel like doing some sketching, something that's alive."

"Where?"

"Eneko, do you mind if we use your apartment this morning, maybe your bedroom, then we won't be disturbing anyone?"

"That's not a problem. Maybe get Viv to sit as well, get her mind off things."

"Excellent idea, okay Zoriona, let's get the things and we can get out of Eneko and George's hair."

George said she would help, so I made a phone call to Lavina. "You're early Eneko, I've only just arrived. There was a traffic jam on Smithdown Road, something exploded at Edgehill Station."

"Yeah, I heard, Lavina, can you send me some of the underwear that George chose last week in black and red? Yeah, good. And something different that would fit Begonia and her friend, Zoriona. Oh! You met Zoriona, did you, okay? well you know the sizes, yeah as soon as you can, please."

The girls returned with the artist's materials and went into the bedroom. George left them to it and went into the kitchen and made some coffee. Viv came in, she still looked shocked, George gave her a hug and Begonia shouted, "Viv, come on, we're in Eneko's bedroom."

George smiled. "Bee's idea of therapy, a life session. You don't have to if you don't want to."

Viv smiled, "No, that's a wonderful idea." And went into the bedroom.

George looked at me. "I wonder how Sugar got on last night?"

"He'll ring when he's got everything in order. I imagine he'll have a lot on his plate."

A knock at the door. It was Lavinia's courier. I thanked the young lad and dropped him a couple of quid.

"More bloody shopping, En?"

"Yeah, underwear for each of you, but not for Viv. I thought that would be out of order, but I have a scarf for her. It's in the drawer where I keep your underwear!"

"My underwear! What's this, confession time?"

"You know what I mean! Now, can you please give the girls their stuff? Yours is in there as well, the larger set!"

I ducked as George threw an imaginary coffee pot at me. She laughed and went to see the girls. I heard whoops of appreciation and cries of "Thanks, boss." And then a blast of Basque from Zoriona which asked how did I know her size?

George came back out. "I'm going to leave them to it. Let's have a wander, figure out what to do about the wage's robbery and let Sugar sort out what's left of them."

We walked off down the lane. The overnight rain had just about stopped, and the air felt clean and smelt fresh. I told George she and Begonia were going to stay with me for a week. She put her head to one side and said, "Why?"

I explained that when Binns was doing up Viv's old apartment for Zoriona, he'd do hers and Begonia's up at the same time and they could help with the fittings and fabrics. George grabbed my arm, kissed me, and said, "And I'll get Sammy to help. He's superb at colour schemes."

Chapter 17—Tidying up loose ends

"Good, he seems like an affable lad and smart, too. You know I think Begonia's exhibition is going to go well, and I wouldn't be surprised if someone took it to Bilbao. People there take that kind of art very seriously. She might even become famous. I hope you are going to handle that?"

"You know the same thoughts have been going through my head for a while now, but hey! It's all so very exciting, it's been a hell of a couple of years. Come on, let's annoy Ruby."

Ruby was flat out in the Kardomah as usual, George gestured we had time, and we settled into a corner to observe the crowd. After about 5 minutes Ruby came over with coffee, "Morning, can I get you something to eat?"

"No, we're good, but I have got some news for you, Bee is waiting to do your portrait next week and then it'll be in her exhibition at the art college, you'll be famous!"

"As long as the customers don't expect me to serve coffee, starkers then I'll enjoy the fame and fortune. Maybe my old man will show a bit more interest, now that the whole town can see what's on offer."

We laughed, Ruby went back to the counter, the phone rang. She held up the receiver and pointed to me, I got up and went over.

Sugar was on the line, he sounded knackered. "Eneko, what a night! We got the gang at Canada Dock, they were trying to bring in an awful lot of drugs, a right beggar's banquet, plus rather a lot of explosives, didn't even know there was a market for that. So that was a result."

"The Edgehill deal, God knows what happened there, witnesses said they heard gunshots and then boom! Witnesses said that the freight car was apparently packed with drugs hidden in cans of fruit, while the next car contained explosives. With all that and bullets flying around, disaster was inevitable, and that's what we got. We've found seven bodies all in a right state, impossible to recognise although one body had a webbed finger! The word from the street is the rest of the gang have left, but for how long we'll see."

"So is the big boss happy?"

"His lordship is very happy, I even shared a large, top-of -the-shelf, scotch with him for breakfast. Now if we could get a lead on this wage holdup I may decide to retire and rest on my laurels."

"We have heard nothing yet, but you'll be the first to know when we do, mate!"

"Good, say hi to the boss."

I handed the phone back to Ruby; George was waiting with eyebrows raised.

"Seven bodies, one of them is Joe Briggs, the rest by the sound of things are unrecognizable. It seems there were guns, ammunition, and explosives in the next freight car. A disaster waiting to happen. The police raid at Canada dock proved to very successful, they found a lot of drugs, guns, and explosives, Sugar is not sure about the explosives. So that gang will be behind bars for a long stretch and, according to Sugar, many gang members have left town. So that means we can turn all our resources to finding the van robbers and their cash and then deliver them to Sugar."

"And I thought the van robbers were going to be the easiest to find and sort out, you just never know, eh! En. But I think we should show Eddie our appreciation of his opportune intervention."

"I'll see he gets it later today."

We meandered back to base, the girls were still sketching, and Binns and Tank were still checking, so far nothing. I thought we were going to need a bit of luck to find any evidence to put the Garston boys out of action other than just turning up and getting into a dogfight. In the meantime, it was all about getting Frank back in place and Binns, Viv, and twins up on part of the top floor. The next few days, nothing happened except for the apartments taking shape. Binns invited

George and I over to see the new flat on the top floor. It looked stunning, Viv would be ecstatic! George was very complimentary about the decor and furniture and the overall colour scheme.

Binns said, "Young Sammy, what a bloody find, he knows his onions we're going to be busy doing up interiors."

George checked everything out including the bedroom and then went out to talk to Sammy about Zoriona's place. They had a long conversation with Sammy drawing some designs in a sketchbook. George came back and said to Binns, "Zee can stay with Bee and me while you're doing up her place, Sammy's got some ace designs, I'm going to have a chat with them tonight as I believe Vee is moving out tomorrow! When are you going to tell her, Binns?"

Binns said, "I'm picking up Frank in an hour, so when we show him his flat, I'll take Viv and the twins upstairs and show them around and then maybe a couple of beers with Frank to celebrate and then get the show on the road tomorrow."

George kissed Binns and gave him a hug. "I'm so happy for you and Vee and the twins, it's brilliant."

I gave Binns a slap on the back, "Same from me, mate."

We headed back to the office; George was in a thoughtful mood and sat down and started sketching some ideas on a notepad. I went into my apartment and did a bit of tidying up. I heard Viv shout, "Frank," and George and I joined Viv outside the office. Frank waved and Binns drove down to the cooperage and Frank's old office which was now his new flat. He wandered in and stood stock still, he looked shocked to the core. He kissed Viv and shook Binns by the hand, "This is bloody marvellous, you are a conniving pair."

Viv shushed him and got him seated in his new armchair and put the kettle on, he was beaming. Next thing the twins arrived with Tank and raced over to Uncle Frank, but Tank was on hand to stop them leaping all over him and they went into the kitchen and got some biscuits from Viv.

Binns said, "Twins, Viv, you follow me, and they trooped upstairs, after about twenty the twins came flying down, "We've got our own bedrooms, Eneko and it's so smart!"

Viv came down, she was in tears, she hugged George and kissed me on the cheek, "Boss you are... I don't know what to say, except thank you."

Tank was beaming, "Right twins let's get some fish and chips while mum and Uncle Frank are getting settled."

George and I left them to it and went back to the office, George put the bath on and seemed lost in her thoughts. "Eneko, you know after Binns and crew have done up Vee's old place for Zee, would you mind if I redecorated our flat, I'd pay for it of course?"

"It's sorted, George, after Binns has finished Zoriona's place it's your turn, design it any way you like, get Sammy to help you and Begonia. I can't wait to see what you come up with, an Art Deco revival, perhaps?"

"En, sometimes you are just too good to be true, but then I know your flaws, well some of them at least. I must watch out for missing underwear!"

The office door opened, and the Basque girls entered. "Is the bath on, George, I feel grubby today and I've got news." I gave the bath miss and had a shower instead. The girls were still in the tub when I got back into the office. They were laughing at something and then they came out in bathrobes and were looking for a drink. Begonia said, "I wish to announce that the exhibition is on the last Saturday of the month from 11 am to 4 pm."

We all cheered. "And I've got an appointment to sketch a lady at the brewery. I've met her, she's in her fifties and has arms and legs like a wrestler, she's perfect. She will be my last one.

I said, "So how many sketches are you going to exhibit?"

"With the last lady that'll make it 12."

George said, "A nice even number, can't wait. Have you had any interest in your articles, Zee?"

"Yes, the Echo is going to publish a guide this Saturday and would you believe, two newspapers in France and two in Spain are going to publish the story."

George said, "En and I have got news, Frank is back and loves his flat; Viv and the twins are over the moon about their new apartment. It looks superb. And Binns is redecorating Viv's flat for Zee."

Zoriona looked shocked, "That's incredible, I don't know what to say."

"There's nothing to say, you're part of the exiled Basque society, so you must have somewhere of your own to stay. And you can monitor George and Begonia for me."

We settled down to some food and wine to celebrate, new flats, new art exhibitions, and future... The evening finished up with everyone merry but ready for bed. The next few days went with little happening. Binns was getting on with Zoriona's apartment and the girls were back and forth with their ideas, young Sammy was almost a permanent fixture with his plans and colour schemes. I was not getting anywhere with the wage robbers, neither was Sugar. I wondered if they were disciplined, since I hadn't heard any stories of them throwing money around or driving flashy new cars. Tank hadn't heard a dickey bird; the Garston boys were lying low.

Zoriona moved into her flat and we were all invited to a party at her place, the apartment looked amazing, almost Art Deco. Sammy was there and congratulated by everyone. In the living room above the fireplace was a Begonia sketch of Viv, Jasmin, Zoriona, and George it looked superb. While they were doing up George and Begonia's place, Begonia stayed with Zoriona as she had room to work, and George stayed with me as we could work out each morning without disturbing no one.

Begonia was up to her eyes with her exhibition and Zoriona was writing lots for her for various newspapers, English, French and Spanish, nothing in Basque yet but she was hoping. So, George was left with her designing mate, Sammy, to come up with most of the ideas for the flat. Begonia nipped in now and again and said she thought it was looking wonderful.

Chapter 18 The exhibition takes shape

One evening George had put the bath on and I was enjoying its relaxing powers when we were joined by the Basque girls. It felt like we hadn't bathed together for ages, so there were lots of stories and jokes. Begonia jumped up out of the bath and sat on the side.

"I forgot to tell you I went to the brewery to sketch Gertie. I turned up and went to the bottling plant where she worked. She oversees loading the lorries, Jesus! She is so strong; she picked me up like I was a child and asked me where I wanted her to pose. I looked around and in one of the corners were a couple of beer barrels. You know those huge ones, so I said there, please."

"Next thing, she undressed and sat on the barrel. The other women cheered. So, I started sketching. She looked fantastic, shoulders like a coal miner, legs that could crush iron bars. She had huge breasts and a magnificent stomach, some interesting scars, but she was proud of her well-lived body. She sat there, and I sketched for 2 hours non-stop, with her only occasionally shouting out orders to her workers. I said I'd finished the basic outline and Gertie, and her workers gathered round. Gertie said she loved it and kissed me on the cheek. Quite a few of the other girls said they'd sit for me anytime. It was a brilliant day; I think a load of them will come to the exhibition."

George laughed, "That sounds brilliant. I can't wait to see the finished work. And if you like sketching big, powerful women, I'll introduce you to Blodwen, who works on the farm next to mine. She's an amazing woman. In fact, you could do a series of women working in the countryside."

"Wow, I love it, George. Zoriona could write a story about them."

These girls were so full of ideas, I felt inadequate. So much energy and life and here I was sitting in a bath with them, perfect. I got out first and left them to it. I changed and said I was nipping out for a pint. In the White Star it was lively for a weeknight. Maisy was behind the bar.

She put a pint in front of me and said, "En, our Maggie wants a word with you but, you know what she's like, doesn't say much."

Chapter 19—Another world

I spotted Maggie sitting by the hearth, staring into space. I went over and sat next to her. "Alright Maggie?"

She looked startled. "Oh, it's you En, you alright?"

"Yeah, all good. You look deep in thought."

She looked at me, smiled. "I never thanked you for sorting those bloody pimps out and frightening them out of my life."

I just smiled.

"Trouble is, I've got another favour to ask, but I feel I'm being bloody cheeky, but here goes. I've got a couple of mates, who are still on the game, and they both have kids, one is 15 and the other is 13. They're both terrified as the kids have been going out at night and staying out and coming home looking wrecked, she spotted some guys dropping them off and went out to have a word about the kids being too young and one bloke got out slapped her around a bit and put a bloody knife against her throat and warned her off, otherwise he'd slice her up good. She's bloody petrified. She thinks the kids are getting hooked on drugs and good knows what else they are getting into."

"Do you know where the kids go?"

"No idea, but I was thinking of following them one night, but my nerve failed me."

"Okay Maggie, don't say a word to your mates, just write their names and addresses and leave it to me, alright." Maggie went over to the bar, got a piece of paper off Maisy, and wrote something down. She folded the paper, came back over, handed me the paper, smiled, and kissed me on the cheek.

"I'll see you soon, Maggie."

I went back to the office, deep in thought. Somebody should sort out these evil bastards. The Basque girls had gone back to Zoriona's place so that Begonia could do some work on her sketches and Zoriona could get some facts for her story. George was making some coffee. She

84

reached for the Remy and held it up. "Yes, to both, George. Can we have a chat?"

"Sure En, what's up?"

I told her of my chat with Maggie and the kids going missing.

"En, you know I've had similar conversations with Maisy and Ruby, there's lots of rumours, child prostitution seems to be a growing concern."

"Well, we need to do something about it. Let's get Tank onboard and see what he's heard."

"Okay, but he spends all his spare time on doing up a hot rod, he's friendly with an American guy who lives up near his uncle Ted's garage, he's got a hot rod, and they have a club at Burton Wood, so Tank goes there sometimes and mixes with the greasers! Jasmin said his hot rod is looking superb, and he's getting Bee to design the motive he wants. It's going to look wild."

"Okay, I've got the names of these girls and their mums from Maggie, so we need to get cracking. I'm going to ring Tank; these kids live down the Dingle way."

I rang Tank and explained my idea and how we should go about it. He agreed and said he'd got some news as well, maybe about the Garston boys. He said he'd be around in an hour.

George and I got ready. George said, "I'm going to take a pistol, just in case it gets hairy."

I said, "Grab my beretta as well."

We heard Tank's Zephyr and went out. Tank said, "George, put your leather jacket on. Eneko, you jump in the back. George, you sit next to me, you can be my Judy, alright."

George laughed, "Does that mean we get to go 'necking"

Tank laughed and gunned the engine. We squealed out of the lane and headed down the dock road and out towards the Dingle.

Tank said, "We need to be conspicuous; the Garston boys are into their cars, someone may bite."

I directed Tank to an address in the Dingle. I got out and knocked on the door. A slim, brassy blonde opened the door. She looked at me. I said, "I'm Maggie's mate. You wanted a word."

"Come on in." She shut the door and took me through to the kitchen. A clean, modern one.

"Has Maggie explained?"

"Yeah, she said you were worried about your daughter, and you thought there were dodgy characters chasing young girls."

"My kid has gone out now. Some right piece of work just picked her up in his car. I thought it was him again when I saw your car 'cos it's just like yours."

"Any idea where they go?"

"Somewhere on the way to Garston, but where? I don't know."

"Okay, don't say a word to anyone, but we'll check it out."

"Thanks, Maggie said you were a nice guy."

"Okay, I'll do my best."

I jumped back in the car and explained what I'd just been told. Tank hit the throttle, and we buzzed up the street and went through Aigburth.

Tank said, "keep your eyes peeled for a Ford Zephyr that looks like this. I saw one a few weeks back. It's likely the same one."

We cruised along but we couldn't see any sign of a similar car, we'd almost reached Garston when a young bloke waved and shouted, "Alright Bean." Tank slowed down and the bloke came over, "Sorry mate I thought you were Bean."

Tanks laughed, "Somebody's got taste like me, then?"

The bloke laughed, "Just like Bean Roberts, he drives a motor very similar to yours. You'll have seen him around. He lives down on the industrial estate near the river."

"It would be nice to catch up and have a chat about engines. Thanks, mate."

We drove off and continued towards the centre of Garston. Tank pulled up in a pub car park.

"I've got Binn's night camera, so I reckon George and I will do a recce. Eneko, you stay in the car, your clothes don't fit in with the locals."

George laughed, kissed me on the cheek, "I think you're still cool, En."

I stayed in the car and waited. The street was dead. They were away for about 40 minutes and then I saw them making their way back up the street. They got in.

"Jesus En, we are going to be very busy sorting out those bastards. Tank spotted the car parked in a yard next to an old warehouse. We could hear music and voices coming from the second floor. The lighting was awful, so we slipped up the stairs. We went through to an empty room opposite them. The windows were grimy, so it was difficult to see much, but someone switched on a light in an adjacent room. In the light, we could see a few old mattresses, 5 or 6 blokes, loads of needles and about the same number of girls all in various stages of undress, some having sex and some just drinking and staring at the walls. But En, some girls, looked young, maybe eleven or twelve. Their parents would go crazy knowing what the girls are up to."

"We need to get photos. It seems the parents are being threatened, but that doesn't make too much sense. You'd have thought if the dads knew they'd round kicking up a real fuss."

"Eneko, you know Jasmin has been telling me about child abuse. She reckons some of these so-called homes are letting the kids go out and are being paid off. But you're right, let's get some evidence then we can show your mate, Sugar. I know he'll go ballistic."

"Right, let's get back to base, get Binns and his surveillance gear. I'll get in touch with Sugar; George, you have another chat with Maggie and Ruby. And then tomorrow night we can meet up and see where we are at."

Tank said, "Okay. But before I forget. You know I'm doing up a hot rod with Uncle Ted and Brian. But also, with a guy who lives round the corner from the garage, he's an aircraft mechanic on the base at Burton Wood. We get on. He loves talking engines, and he's brilliant for getting parts. But he mentioned that a guy in a car like mine had been asking around about guns. He didn't know if he'd got any, but there's a lot of stuff just lying around."

George said, "Do you think the Garston boys could be involved in more than just robbing vans?"

"I think anything is possible right now. Let's just follow the plan for the moment and see what information we can gather."

Tank dropped us off. George was in a thoughtful mood. She was scowling. "Bastards like that ill-treating all those kids. This need sorting out, En. I'd better give you my pistol back. I may get an urge to shoot people! See you in the morning for a tough workout."

I poured myself a large Remy. Maybe Jasmin was right. Young kids out and about with no form of parental control. Maybe because parents didn't exist. I needed an in to find out about children's homes and how they were run. That would take a bit of teasing out. Sugar was the man to ask. He could point me in the right direction.

I wanted to keep the police out of this investigation until I had these bastards by the short and curlies. Sleep didn't come easy, and I awoke feeling angry and nervy. I needed a workout. I'd just got started when George arrived. She said little, just got stuck into the workout and was kicking holes in the punchbag. I somehow felt the same. We finished, George went into the shooting gallery, and I heard her gun coughing. I left her to it. I showered and got changed. Viv had the coffee going when I entered the office, "Morning boss, toast?"

"Please Viv."

George came in, "Hi Viv, toast for me too, please."

We ate and drank in silence; Viv was typing away in her usual efficient way. George signalled she was going for a walk. She looked mad; I knew what was bothering her, but she'd taken things to heart after seeing those kids last night. My chat with Sugar couldn't wait. I rang his office, and his secretary answered, "He's in. I'll put you through."

Sugar came on the line. "Morning Eneko, what's up? This is a bit early for you."

"Sugar, I've come across some nasty shit. I need an hour of your time for a chin wag."

"Okay, Eneko, lunch time at the Phil. I've got a meeting up that way this morning."

"Thanks Sugar, see you later."

The phone rang. Viv answered, "Yes he is." And handed me the phone. A friendly Basque voice entered my ears. "Eneko, how are you? I've been thinking about your idea for a Basque evening, how about we combine it with launching Begonia's exhibition, I'll lay on the food and drink at the gallery, and we can take some photos and Zoriona can write an article, and I will send it to my friends in Bilbao."

"Pedro Bengoa, you are becoming a real wily old fox. Talk about milking the situation."

Pedro laughed, "Then I take it you agree with me, good? I'll get on to the gallery and organise some intercultural material with the Consul."

"So, you're moving in diplomatic circles now?"

"You know the answer to that, my young friend. See you soon."

I smiled to myself as I hung up. Pedro was a clever, an ingenious man. Using art to depoliticise a situation took brains and patience. That was Pedro Bengoa in a nutshell.

Chapter 20—Gerty comes to call

I idled away the morning jotting down some questions I wanted to ask Sugar. And things Tank and Binns could work on. I went into my apartment to use the bathroom and on my way out I could hear a loud voice, not Viv's. I entered the office. A large, powerful woman was talking to Viv. She saw me, stuck her hand out and gripped mine and said, "I'm Gertie, your girlfriend did my portrait."

"Oh, nice to meet you. I'm Eneko."

"Is Georgina in?"

"You mean George? Sorry, she's out now. Can I help?"

"You can tell her I called; she's just stopped me ma from getting robbed. A couple of toe rags tried to steal her handbag, but your George flattened the pair of them. I'd like to buy her a drink and say thanks."

"Is your mum alright, Gertie?"

"Yeah, she's fine. Take more than a couple of toe rags to put the wind up her. She's at the brewery having a cup of tea."

The office door opened, George walked in, Gertie took one look at her, smiled, and picked her up like she was a feather, kissed her on the cheek, "George isn't it, well aren't you a sight for sore eyes. That was me, ma, you helped earlier. You look strong. The lady in the newspaper shop said you mangled those toe rags. Come on, let's have a drink and a natter."

George tried to say something, but nothing came out, so I said, "Good idea Gerty, the White Star is just around the corner."

Gerty said, "Come on, George, move your rear end."

They left, Viv started laughing, "George has got another admirer. I'm going to get fit and start kicking people. It's the only way to go."

"Jesus, you wouldn't argue with Gerty. She's built like a tank, a proper one, makes our Tank, look like an armoured car."

"Jesus! Boss, I feel sorry for her husband. If there is one, that is. I almost said to Gerty, I didn't recognise you with your clothes on, but I decided not to."

"Smart move, Viv, you live to fight another day. Okay, I'm going to make a move; I'm meeting Sugar at the Phil if you need me."

"Okay boss, say hi."

I bowed and went on my way. The air was getting chilly, soon the fires would be on, and the coal fires would herald the start of the smoggy season. But for now, the chill felt refreshing, and my new lightweight overcoat felt perfect for the day. I walked up past the Adelphi and turned up past the YMCA and then turned right into Hope Street and along to the Phil. I was early, so I grabbed a table near the window and away from the bar. The waitress came over and I ordered a sherry. I took out my notebook and had a look at the questions I wanted to ask Sugar. My sherry arrived and with it, Sugar. I ordered him a pint.

"What's up Sherlock?"

"Okay, Sugar, what do you know about the orphanage situation in the city and using the kids as prostitutes?"

"Jesus Eneko, no foreplay, just straight to it. The situation is a minefield. Do know how many kids became orphans or went missing during and right after the war? It's a grey area, there're all kinds of rumours, but nothing concrete except the occasional tip off. There are loads of orphanages. I'll send you through the details and if you need any help or hear anything reliable, I'll be there."

"I know, Sugar, but I've been hearing some awful rumours and I'm going to check on them and I'll let you know."

"Okay, but be careful. Anything new on our van robbers?"

"Another reason, I wanted to have a chat. Tank is friendly with an American serviceman off the base at Burtonwood. They are both into Hot Rods and Tank is going to check with him if anyone has been asking about guns, you never know."

"Okay, the drug gang turned out to be a result, once we got them locked up and started questioning. A couple of them cracked as they knew the lads who got blown to smithereens up at Edgehill. It got them talking, so we got some proper information on what these gangs are trying to do and who the top villains are. The boss is happy for the moment."

"Okay mate, I'll look forward to getting anything you have on orphanages and then I'll try to get as much info as I can before getting back to you."

"Okay, let's have one for the road, then I can get back and finish the meeting I was at."

We supped up and Sugar went back to his meeting. I wandered back to the office. Viv was on the phone, still no sign of George, so I made a coffee. I pointed to Viv. She nodded.

Viv put the phone down, "That was Tank, he's been chatting to his American mate. He's hoping to come up with a name later today."

"Good. We need a bit of luck. No sign of George yet?"

"No, she must be getting drunk with Gerty. When Gerty says drink, you drink."

"How's the apartment?"

"Boss, I still can't believe it. It's heaven, Helen is so over the moon she's started talking nine to the dozen, she's even more of a chatterbox than her brother, who now lives downstairs with Frank. And the bit I love is, it brought me to tears the other day. Helen asked Binns if she could call him dad. I thought he was going to cry as well, but he just nodded and ruffled her hair, and she raced down to tell Frank and Eric."

I smiled. "That must be an enormous relief, Viv. Has Eric said anything yet?"

"He likes Binns being called dad, too. I think it'll all be good as long as I don't call him dad as well."

That made me laugh. I was still laughing when George walked in. She looked a little less angry than this morning, but not much. She looked at us.

Viv said, "Did you keep up with Gerty's drinking?"

George laughed. "Are you bloody kidding? She's unbelievable, what a woman. Eneko, I've got some news, we need to chat. Viv, not hiding this from you, but it's nasty stuff and you don't need to be hearing this right now, okay?"

Viv nodded, "Whatever you say, George."

So George and I trooped into the apartment. George said, "Sit down En. I was having a drink with Gerty. She thanked me and said if ever I needed anything to just call her. She loved the posing bit, and she thought Bee was an ace. Then she asked me why I looked so down in the mouth."

"I didn't know what to say, but I mentioned orphans and orphanages. She put her arm around me and said come with me. We went off to the brewery to see her mum. Her mum had recovered from this morning. She looks like a chip off the old block. She kissed me on the forehead and the other women gave me slaps on the back. Gerty, her mum, and I went into Gerty's office. She explained to her mother what I'd said. Ethel gave me a look and then told me that Gerty was orphaned. Her mum had died after WW1, and her father died at the battle of the Somme. But Ethel knew Gerty's mum and so she went along to adopt her. She said it was a nightmare. Bureaucracy gone mad. That's when she heard of some dodgy goings on. Later in life, she tried to help with kids who were left. But she said that during WW11, some stories made her hair stand on end."

George brought a cardboard file out of her bag and emptied it out. Ethel had put all the names of the homes in south Liverpool and put stars by the names of the homes she thought were dodgy.

I looked at George. "This has affected you, hasn't it?"

"Yeah, I met kids from Liverpool in the war and some stories I heard would make you weep, so now if I can do anything to stop this I will, no matter what."

"Okay George, I'm with you 100% and so is everyone. I've just had a conversation with Sugar and he's sending everything he's got on the subject and the right people to talk to about this problem. And Tank is checking things out with his mate from the base. But, in the meantime, George, we need to be cool and collected on this one. Rational minds, not muddled thinking."

She nodded. I gave her a big hug, and she kissed me on the cheek. She got up, "More coffee, En?"

"Please."

"Okay, so this is what we've got: Ethel's information and her contacts with the council; Sugar is sending us his info; Binns is doing his undercover photography; Tank is trying to get names to match cars and guns! Meanwhile, you and I are going to collate all this info and come up with a plan to eradicate these bastards."

"Okay En, my job is going to see Ethel's contacts at the council with Ethel. You liaise with Sugar, Tank, and Binns and set up a meeting for tomorrow evening and see what we've got."

George went back out into the office, and I heard Viv saying goodbye. I ran the bath, assuming George would need it; she appeared distressed. Back in the office, George was sitting on the couch, head in her hands, sobbing. I put my arms around her, and she put her head on my shoulder and didn't move for a while. The phone rang. It was Begonia. "Eneko, Zoriona and I are at the gallery. We'll be here for a while. Tell George I'll be back about 9 pm, okay?"

"Yeah, see you later. That was Begonia. She's working late at the gallery, back about 9 pm. But now it's bath time."

George just sat on the little stool and didn't even wash herself, so I turned on the shower and scrubbed her back and legs, shampooed her hair and helped her into the bath. She didn't say a word, just stayed still in the water. I got out and left her in the water. Got changed, poured a couple of Rémys, and grabbed one of my dressing gowns. Pulled George out of the bath into the dressing gown and onto the couch. I handed her a glass of Remy and made her take a couple of sips. She sat quietly for a while. I put on the radio, and we sort of half listened to Tony Hancock. George finished her Remy, so I poured another one. She smiled and started sipping. A bit later, I heard the phone ring. Begonia said, "Eneko, I'm knackered. Tell George I'll see her for coffee in the morning."

George was out, so I picked her up and put her into my bed and made up the couch for myself. In the morning, I heard the knock on the door. Begonia came in. She saw the look on my face and went through to the apartment. She joined George in bed and gave her a big hug and got her up. "George, and what are you like? No underwear!"

George said, "I hope you're not complaining."

"Coffee and toast, ladies?"

Yes, please, came the reply. The office opened and Viv arrived. "Did I hear the magic words?"

"You did, Viv."

"Then leave it to me, boss."

Chapter 21—Information gathering

George reappeared, dressed, and looking better, she kissed me on the cheek, "Thanks for last night, En."

Viv looked up, "Ears closed, honest."

George went over to Viv, kissed her on the cheek, "Get to work Miss Vee, we've lots to do today. In fact, I'd like you to come with Ethel and me to the council offices. You can take notes. Is that okay En?"

"Yeah, I'm going to be in the office all day getting a grip on all the information coming in."

Begonia said, "It sounds like a hive of activity. I'll leave you to it. Be around for a bath tonight. See you."

"Right Viv let's get ready, we're picking up Ethel in about half an hour, so let's go by taxi. Can you organise that, please? I think Ethel has got us some appointments. If not, we'll play it by ear."

"Okay, En, I'll call you if anything dramatic happens, if not see you at bath time. And I hope the information gathering goes well."

The taxi arrived, and the girls left. Another taxi arrived, a load of paperwork from Sugar. I sat down and started putting the info into some sort of logical order. Not straight forward, but some things stood out. The office door opened, and Binns and Tank came in. "Morning Eneko, you look busy, mate."

"Hi lads, yeah, just trying to put the paperwork in some sort of order, some interesting stuff. You got anything?"

Binns passed me some film canisters. "That's pretty much all of them at the old warehouse, including the kids. Jesus, some kids look a real mess."

Tank said, "Eneko, I could do with a coffee, mate."

"Sorry lads, would you like some toast as well?"

"No, but coffee would hit the spot. Eneko, I met up with my American mate, and we went out to the base in my car. At the base, Errol introduced me to some of his hot rod mates and. Another soldier

96

came over and looked at my car and asked if it was mine. I said it was, and he said he'd told my buddy not to come back, as asking about weapons was not cool. Errol explained I was looking for a guy who drives a similar ride. The guy apologised but said his car was a dead ringer for mine. So, I waited around for a while with Errol, but nothing came to light. Errol was sure that our mate had got himself some weapons, as the security had been lax. But it didn't sound like he'd be back again."

"Okay, I'll develop the films. Binns, can you do another recce during the day and see if you can spot anything else, maybe kids coming back and forth? Tank, I'd like you to check out two homes. One is called Strawberry Fields. It's just past Calderstones Park, but the kids may talk about other kids, you know. And there's another one called Nazareth House and the kids there are called Nazis! You couldn't write this. These homes seem fine, but maybe the kids will talk to you about other homes they may have been in."

"Okay, Eneko, when do we all meet up?"

"Tomorrow at about 8 pm, here. George and Viv should have information from the council and I'm working through stuff from Sugar, which I should have ready by then, okay?"

"We're on it Eneko, see you tomorrow."

I spent the rest of the day going through details about homes, some dodgy characters, and pure rumour. I spoke with Sugar twice, and he was very informative. But I thought he hadn't, or the police hadn't spent a lot of time investigating rumours and speculation about kids in orphanages. I made another coffee, scribbled down some more ideas, and tried to think. Dead end, but the timely intervention of George and Viv, who'd returned from meetings with the council, saved me. I put the coffee on.

"Jesus En, that was awful. Can you pour out some, Remy? My head is on fire."

George looked pale. She put her Remy down and Viv poured another.

I said, "Okay, let's hear all about it."

Viv motioned for George to speak. "Okay, we went off with Ethel to see a couple of ladies who oversee some orphanages in south Liverpool. They explained that truancy was a big problem, kids nipping out during the day from the homes or, more worryingly, at night. The kids have next to nothing, so the offer of free fags, chocolate for the young ones and nylons and clothes for the older girls is always going to turn heads. The girls are an easy target, and although the people in charge, the police, and councillors, won't admit it, it's almost impossible to police. However, some of the homes have noticed girls looking gaunt and vacant. They suspect drugs, but it's hard to prove. A couple of homes have got some dodgy looking people working in them. I've got the list, two in Garston. Ethel's ex-colleague told us she thinks prostitution is rife. She also reckoned pornographic photos were now in vogue. She showed us a few, not nice."

"So do we think the Garston boys are involved in organised prostitution, or are just recruiting girls for themselves?"

Chapter 22—Master plan

Viv said, "Boss, I don't think those lowlifes have the brains to organise an operation like this. I think they're just part of a much bigger picture. They're just thugs, nasty bastards."

"En, I agree, but they still need a bloody tough lesson. This needs to be stopped and word about their demise to be broadcasted all over the city."

They both looked very serious and done in. I kept my peace.

Viv said, "I'm going to love you and leave and save Frank from the twins. They'll be back from school by now."

"Yeah, Okay Vee, thanks for coming today. See you in the morning."

"You okay, George?"

"Yeah, I'm fine, En, just mad, frustrated and determined to sort those bastards out once and for all. I'll put the bath on and try to soak my frustrations away."

"Okay, by tomorrow evening Binns and Tank should have some more info, and then we can go to work."

Begonia and Zoriona arrived just in time for the bath. I left them to it. I thought they would cheer George up, some female chat. I rang Tank, Jasmin answered, "Hi Eneko, you, okay?"

"Yeah fine, Jasmin. I've got a question. Have you heard anything about an increase in drug addiction in young girls?"

"Yeah, Tank asked me the same question this morning, so I've checked. The answer is yes, and there is also an increase in venereal infections in young girls. Not that the two things go hand in hand, but there is usually a connection."

"Thanks Jasmin, could you get Tank to ring when he gets in, please?"

I put the phone down. I could hear laughter coming from the bathroom. Begonia was ecstatic about the upcoming exhibition, and

Zoriona had the wonderful news that both French and Spanish newspapers had contacted them. We sat around, shared a bottle of wine and some sandwiches before the girls left and went next door. George got ready for bed, and I settled down on the couch. The phone rang. I picked up.

"Eneko, some idiots are trying to break into the empty flat. I've called Tank as well."

"Okay, whatever you do, stay inside Zoriona's apartment."

George was all ears. I looked at George. "Let's go. Stay with me."

We raced outside. We heard the roar of a car engine and then nothing. Tank appeared at the top of the lane and came running down. "That car was the Garston boys."

We went to the front of the apartment. They hadn't broken in, but the door had been damaged and on it was a message, held in place with a knife 'Keep your nose out of our business, George.'

George ripped it to pieces and said, "That's it. I'm going to sort those bastards out right now."

Tank grabbed her. "George, whoa! We'll get them, but we need to be cold-blooded about this. Going off half-cocked is going to get us nowhere. And I know Binns has got some more interesting info, so let's talk about it in the morning rather than tomorrow night, okay, Eneko?"

"Sounds good. I'll have the coffee ready. George, you go back to bed. Tank and I will have a word with the girls and put their minds to rest. I'll be back in a minute."

The girls looked worried, but we quickly calmed them down. Tank offered them a place to stay if they were still anxious, but the girls said they were okay. So, Tank and I exchanged glances and went back to our homes.

George was in the bedroom when I got back. I said, "Goodnight." She didn't say a word but pulled me into bed with her, wrapped her body around me, kissed me on the cheek, and went to sleep.

I slept like a log; I awoke alone, but I could smell coffee and toast. 8 am! I heard Viv, she was laughing about something. I dressed and went into the office.

"Morning ladies, the coffee smells wonderful." George was still in her dressing gown, and she appeared calmer, almost serene.

"Hi boss, you look like you slept well." She glanced at the couch, which didn't look like anyone had slept in it, and looked at George. Who looked right back at her with those eyebrows well arched? "Vee, have you finished typing up the report from yesterday?"

"I'm on it, George."

George went into the bedroom to get changed. Viv kept her eyes down and typed away.

George reappeared, "Right Viv, you and I need to get everything we learned from yesterday on paper now, as Binns and Tank are coming around for a meeting. So, I'll talk it out and you just type it down, but bullet points only, okay?"

"Gotcha, George."

I rang Sugar, who was just on his way out. I mentioned that we'd made some interesting discoveries, and we'd keep him up to date with what we were doing. He said he'd catch up later this evening. The girls were busy making notes when Binns and Tank arrived. Viv stopped and put the coffee on. We all gathered around the coffee table, coffee in hand, Viv and George with notes.

Binns started, "I've got photos of most of them, kids. I followed the two girls back to a home in Garston at midnight. A big bloke opened the door, they gave him an envelope, and they went in. In the warehouse, they have a room set up for taking pictures and a room for developing. They have cars which take girls to different locations and then they pick them up later. Most of the girls are then driven back to either of the three homes. A few seem to be permanent fixtures at the warehouse. I followed one car to another broken down warehouse in

Garston and they were supplying drugs and picking up money. It looks like a drug racket, a prostitution ring, and a nice line in dirty photos."

We all looked at Tank, "Like I said the other day, I'm pretty sure these bastards have weapons and connections, but with who or where I'm not sure. But I checked out some homes in south Liverpool, played football with some lads or talked about hot rods. They loved my car. They mentioned two of the places Binns saw girls delivered back to and a couple of names of nasty bastards who seem to oversee the comings and goings of the girls. It's too big a task to get them all implicated and get the law on to them. I think, like George, we go in hard and batter them and leave enough clues and evidence for the law to have a look at. Maybe some nasty bastards at the homes could meet up with an accident!"

"Okay, but we need to make sure none of the kids are going to get hurt. Can we take them down outside the warehouse?"

"I think that's going to be difficult, Eneko. We could take out the drug dealing side of the business away from the warehouse, but the rest is difficult. Binns and I think the time to strike is after midnight when most of the young girls are back at their homes."

George nodded, "I agree. Let's make sure we get the hard core of the gang and then leave the dregs for the police."

"When?"

Binns, George, Viv, and Tank looked at me.

"No time like the present," said Viv.

"Okay, I'm with you. Let's meet up tonight here at 10 pm and in the meantime, I'll develop all the film and make sure copies are on Sugar's desk tomorrow morning. We'll use two vehicles tonight; George goes with me, and we go armed to the teeth."

Binns said, "I've got a plan for the place, so we'll take separate floors. They should be all back by then. That means 6 or 7, plus a few kids spaced out on drugs, so we should be able to take them out."

We knew what we had to do, so the lads took their leave and George, and I headed down to the cellar to get our gear in shape for this evening. We loaded our weapons, I put two pistols in my jacket and opted for a Kendo stick to add to my armoury. George had her pistol ready and with a silencer attached. I knew both Tank and Binns would have silencers, so we should be able to get the job done. The rest of the day passed, and I'd developed the films before I knew it. Before Viv left, she gave George a big hug and a kiss on the cheek. She waved to me and blew me a kiss. George had rung the girls, and they said they were working late and then they would go straight home. We had another coffee. George had put on her all-black outfit, so had I. We donned our black duffle coats and left the office. Binns had the Land Rovers ticking over; Tank was driving one and George drove ours.

We drove to Garston and parked up on a derelict bomb site about 3 minutes' walk from the warehouse. Nobody out and about tonight. The only sign of warmth, smoking chimneys in the distance. We waited. Binns got out of the Land Rover and went for a recce, dressed in black and with his balaclava on. He reappeared about twenty minutes later. "The cars have just left, taking the girls back to their homes. When they get back, there should be seven of them plus three or four girls doing drugs, by the look of it."

We nodded; Binns went off again. We waited, George got ready, balaclava on, pistol checked silencer on. She looked at me, leant over and tapped me on the head. "Ready?"

"Ready. Let me go up the stairs first but be ready to shoot."

George nodded. Tank got out of his Land Rover, came over, "Okay, it's almost time. Show no mercy. We're dealing with garbage, remember?"

Binns was in the Land Rover. "Okay, everybody is home. The three downstairs are drinking, upstairs is silent, so it's drugs or sex or both. Tank and I will sort out downstairs and then be right behind you on the second floor."

We followed Binns to the warehouse. A big, old, ugly building with open staircases. Binns pointed up a staircase and held up five fingers. George and I raced up the stairs and reached the second floor before we heard all hell break loose downstairs. I went into the room, two idiots with knives jumped at me but I dispatched them with my kendo stick before they had time to get going, out of the corner of my eye I could see three or four girls lying on the mattresses, they looked out of it. As I turned to check out the rest of the room, another bloke was trying to swing a shotgun in my direction. I heard the silencer on George's gun cough four times and the shotgun landed on the floor with our would-be shooter. Tank and Binns came crashing in, looking around. Binns checked the shooter. He was dead. Three girls were like zombies. Another one looked dead, an overdose by the look of it. Binns and Tank tied the two unconscious bodies up, the girls we left. Downstairs, we checked the other three. They were still lying on the floor, bound and gagged. We left the warehouse. Silence, not a sign of life. Binns motioned for us to get back to the Land Rover. He stayed behind to check things and then he was back with us.

"Eneko, ring the police from the call box by the pub on the main road and we'll see you tomorrow morning."

"Will do. See you in the morning."

I rang the police and got my message across. I mentioned drugs and overdoses. George drove back in silence. At the office, I put the bath on to reheat, poured two glasses of Remy, and handed one to George.

"Thanks for taking out the shooter, George."

She raised her glass. "My pleasure. He looked an evil bastard and those girls like zombies and the other one dead. What do you think the police will find?"

"They'll find everything, the cars, the money, and the drugs. With luck, they'll make the connection: orphanages, drugs and prostitution, but I doubt it. Too many vested interests and a lack of accountability."

"Jesus En! So, what do we do?"

"We keep on plugging away and if the police don't take care of things, then we will. We left a big statement there tonight, not for the police, but for the evil bastards behind all this trade. And little by little we'll get them. Sugar will have received all the photos from us, and he'll no doubt be on the case in Garston. Let's see what happens. Let's get changed, put the weapons away, and get a bath."

We trooped downstairs, cleaned, and unloaded the guns, took our black gear off and went upstairs for a bath. In the bath, George and I just relaxed and let the hot water work its magic. After a while George said, "En, I feel nothing about shooting that bastard tonight. Is that wrong?"

"George, it's just the way we compartmentalise things. During the Spanish Civil War, I saw things that I never believed people could do to people. But it's the way it is. Look at Liverpool, it's nine years after WW11 and what do you see, bomb sites, poverty, hunger, and villains trying to lord it over us? Well, we can do our bit. We have no money worries. We've got property and businesses, but that doesn't mean we don't have to try."

We got out of the bath, put on our dressing gowns, and sat on the couch. I awoke to the smell of fresh coffee and singing! George was asleep next to me. I got up and ventured out into the office.

Chapter 23 Viv is full of surprises

"Morning Boss, toast with your coffee?"

"Please, Viv."

"Is George alright, Binns told me all about last night."

"Yeah, she's still asleep."

Viv said, "Morning George, the coffee is on and toast, too."

"Thanks Vee, I'm bloody starving."

Viv had the toast and coffee ready in a flash and started making some more. Viv was a class act. She knew when to say nothing while saying something. She had grown on me.

"You know on the radio this morning it said this could be the last day of decent weather for the rest of the year, so George, I think you should both go for a walk in the park, nice jacket, nice scarf and enjoy plus it'll put you in the right frame of mind for the exhibition tomorrow. And George, I think you should see Bee. I think she's having kittens!"

George looked at Viv. She kissed Viv on the cheek and went out of the office door.

Viv yelled, "George, you're still in your dressing gown with no knickers on."

I laughed, Viv laughed, "The bloody Welsh, eh!"

The phone rang. Viv answered, "Yes he is, big man, I'll put him on."

"Morning, Eneko. I'll pop round and bring you up to date."

Viv looked at me, "I'll put some more coffee on and ring Binns and tell him to come over later, okay?"

"Fine Viv."

As soon as the coffee was ready, Sugar walked in. "Morning, Viv, how's Frank and the twins?"

"Oh! Frank is back moaning a bit, so he's feeling better, and the twins are still the twins. How are you?"

"All good, Viv, thanks."

Sugar sipped his coffee. "I swear your coffee is better than Eneko's, but don't tell him!

Viv laughed, "I'll leave you boys to it. If you want any more coffee, just sing out."

Sugar said, "I got your photos, right bunch of ugly bastards. I've got my lads working on it. Big showdown in Garston last night. It turns out the Garston boys did that payroll robbery. We found most of the money, loads of drugs, and two dead bodies."

I looked at him. George walked in, dressed, kissed Sugar on the cheek. "Morning officer. To what do we owe this privilege?"

"Morning, George, just bringing Eneko up to speed on the payroll robbery. We found the gang's hideout earlier this morning, plus two dead bodies, some zombies, and villains all tied up and nowhere to go. The girls are all young, orphans from Garston way, the dead girl, too. She'd overdosed and the dead guy was a real nutter we've been after for a long time. I've been on to the council about the girls and which homes they're from. No doubt there will be an investigation, so I'll wait and see. But so far everyone is happy, my boss especially as the investigation into the robbery wasn't going too well. So that's it, I'm off, I've got a busy day."

"Okay, Sugar, thanks for bringing us up to date."

"Not a problem, George, and thanks for the coffee, Viv."

"Any time."

Sugar left, and Viv looked at us and then at the door. Against the wall by the door was my kendo stick. George raised her eyebrows. "Who left that there?"

Viv said, "Not sure, but I think it must have been Sugar."

George smiled, "Sugar, eh! As sweet as his name."

"Viv, why not nip home and grab Binns and telephone Tank and then we'll have our meeting?"

Viv nipped off. George looked a little worried.

I said, "How's Begonia?"

"Bee's okay, just stage fright. I gave her the big up-and-at- 'em speech. She's ready and Zee has been a big help."

Viv and the lads came in. Tank said, "It's all over the news, wages robbers detained, drug's girl found dead. Gang leader shot dead. The other robbers were found bound and gagged. The police think it was a fall out between gang members, and they panicked or got disturbed and escaped just before the police arrived. The police say they received an anonymous tip off."

Binns said, "Well, all in a night's work. I don't think there's any way they can link us to the job."

I looked up. Viv shook her head, "Yeah, I think we're in the clear, so far."

George said, "Binns, the apartment is looking fantastic. I love the colour scheme."

"Not my idea, George. That's all down to Sammy. In fact, I'm due up there now to sort out some kitchen appliances and bathroom fittings, so I'll see you all later."

Tank said, "I'm off to sort out a few problems at the warehouse, so if I don't see you later, I'll see you at the exhibition tomorrow."

"You know what, Vee? I think a walk in the park is what I need. Come on En, get your arse in gear, let's go up to Calderstones Park and have a wander."

So, I took Viv's advice and dressed for the occasion, a navy-blue cord suit, dark brown shoes, bought in Spain and a red mohair scarf. Viv nodded her approval, and George gave me a wolf whistle.

"Okay handsome, let's go, you drive."

I drove to the park. The weather looked benign, with still some warmth in the sun, no wind, just a few leaves drifting from the trees to nestle in the bushes or on the road. George took my arm, and we wandered around and after forty twenty minutes, we came to the big, old oak tree. We stood there looking at it. A quaky voice behind us said, "That oak tree is about a thousand years old, you know."

We turned, and an old lady with a mop of white hair, dressed in a vivid red overcoat, was standing, resting her weight on a walking stick.

"I'm eighty-three and my husband asked me to marry him under that tree sixty-two years ago. He passed away five years ago and every year on the anniversary of his marriage proposal, I come and stand by the oak tree and remember, I have such memories. So, I wish you as a young couple a long and happy married life and fond memories."

George said, "Thank you," and kissed the old lady on the cheek. "We'll leave you to your memories."

As we walked back to the car, George had a spring in her step. "That old lady is right. Live for today and remember at your leisure." She grabbed my arm. "Come on, let's get organised for tomorrow and make it a day for Bee to remember."

We drove back. George rang Begonia and said she was off to the gallery to lend a hand. Viv and I exchanged glances. "Boss, I won't say a word about your kendo stick. What good would it do, anyway? Sometimes, too much knowledge is a curse."

I bent forward, kissed her on the cheek, "So how does life go over at the cooperage?"

"Life does very well, thanks. Binns is brilliant, the twins love him to bits and Frank is looking up."

"Okay, Well I think we should close early today; you can get the twins, and I'll get the bath ready for the girls and look at what I'm going to wear tomorrow."

"Okay boss, I'll just nip next door and see what Binns is up to. I know he's trying his best to get George and Bee's place ready as soon as possible. And I also want to see what young Sammy comes up with."

I picked up my kendo stick and put it back in my apartment, went through my wardrobe and picked out my dark charcoal grey suit, black shoes, white shirt, red tie, and red scarf. I prepared the bath; it would be nice and hot by the time the girls got back. I opened some wine, prepared some bread, cheese, and ham for a light supper. The girls turned up, Begonia looked like a nervous wreck, I kissed her on the cheek, "Come on, the water is hot, time to relax, then I'll have some nibbles and wine."

The girls all went into the bathroom. After about ten minutes, George called out, "En, come on, we want to see that cute behind."

I washed and got in the bath. The girls were in excellent form, Begonia relaxed and Zoriona was all smiles. "Eneko, the gallery looks superb, the sketches are all up and they look superb. And I know there's a lot of press people coming tomorrow and some consular staff, not just Spanish but other nationalities, too."

George said, "Time to eat," and the girls got out of the bath and left me to it. Zoriona was looking lovely and content. I hoped she could settle down in this city and be content with her life. The party was in full swing when I entered the office. Begonia was telling us about how she almost dropped the sketch of Gerty! We all laughed. The girls went and look at the apartment before going to bed. I stayed put and poured a Remy for myself and one for George.

George came in laughing, "The place looks amazing. Bee is delighted. She's invited Sammy to the gallery tomorrow. She thinks he'll blush like a beetroot when he sees the sketches, but I think she's mistaken. I think he's very au fait with art and artistic people."

Saturday morning, George was in the shower. I put the coffee on. I heard George shout. "Toast please, En." She came through to the office in her dressing gown and grabbed coffee and toast.

"I'm going to wear black underwear today; you have some tucked away."

"Of course I do, especially as you seem to lose them regularly."

She laughed. "This is all going in my memoirs."

Chapter 24—The big day arrives

We had a leisurely breakfast. George got dressed in one of her French suits with a pencil slim skirt. She looked superb. George complimented me as well. Viv arrived with Binns, who looked sharp in a new suit, which brought a loud wolf whistle from George and a torrent of Welsh from Binns. Viv wowed in a suit with a hat, and little Helen was in a matching outfit. She looked all grown up.

Viv said, "No Eric, he's staying with Uncle Frank. Pictures are for girls!!"

A knock on the door and in walked Tank, dressed in a new Edwardian creation. He looked very sharp. And in came Jasmin, in national dress. She looked wonderful. The colours were brilliant and complimented her jet-black hair. The door opened again, and the Basque girls came in, both dressed in black with red scarves and matching berets. That drew a round of applause from everyone. The taxis arrived, and we set off for the gallery. When we arrived, there were officials and the press in front of the gallery. After a couple of interviews, Begonia went into the gallery, and we all followed. Within minutes, the place was buzzing. Begonia made a quick speech in English, followed by French and Spanish, with just a few words in Basque.

Then the director of the gallery declared the exhibition open, and the sketches uncovered. There was a slight lull, followed by cheers and applause. Begonia looked delighted, and she went to each of the sketches and introduced the models. The washerwoman sketch was first, followed by a lady chimney sweep and a group of dock workers. All the models were there. Next, we went to the ladies who had posed naked. There was terrific interest. Nods of heads towards Jasmin, George, and Zoriona who looked lovely, but another cheer went up for Gerty posing on a beer barrel and Ruby sitting on a table drinking a coffee.

Pedro Bengoa went around to every lady that had posed and presented them with flowers and chocolates. A nice touch. The press were everywhere, flashbulbs popping, and questions being asked. I spotted Eres, she was talking to Ruby, and then she went across and kissed both Begonia and Zoriona. Then one reporter asked Begonia if people could buy copies? Before Begonia could answer, the gallery director said, of course, and pointed to a counter at the back of the room. There was a lot of interest and things got going. With plenty of Spanish wine on offer, it soon became a rather boisterous affair. George was in deep conversation with Sammy and pointing out parts of some sketches. I saw Eres give George a quick kiss on the cheek as she was leaving. By about 3 pm, most people had drifted off. I could see Begonia and Zoriona beaming. It was marvellous for them and for their hard work. I had a feeling Begonia was going to become quite famous. Sugar and Rhian arrived, and they were checking out the sketches.

But my mind had already started drifting back to last night and young drug addicts and their hardships. And those horrible villains who were profiting by it. It made my blood run cold; crime was never far away. I saw George talking to Rhian and pointing my way. I overheard Eres talking to Gerty about posing at the art college, Gerty spotted me and picked me up and sat me down on her lap, "If Eneko poses with me, I'll do it, you could play a tune on that taut rear end."

George and the other girls laughed, and I felt a slap on my rear. And Rhian's voice, "Only one owner, seldom used."

Gerty roared with laughter, drowning out my reply.

About the Author

As Liverpool emerged from the dust of World War 11, so did I. The birth certificate states born in Penny Lane! The years after the war and into the new decade, 1950s, were harsh. Kids with no shoes, mums with ration books, meat was sausages, butter a luxury.

My dad, an ex-Royal Marine, used to take me down to the Mersey to see the trans-Atlantic liners of the day. The buzz of the riverfront with the Liver Buildings behind and the hustle and bustle of freighters, big and small. The Overhead Railway, or the 'Docker's Umbrella', as it was known, provided a view of the entire 7 miles of docks. You could see an entire city of docks with ships coming and going to all four corners of the world—a magnificent sight.

That was the backdrop to my childhood, that and Liverpool FC. My granny lived in Lothar Road, so I used to sneak in for the last 15 mins of each game and then as I got older the Boys Pen. After School I had various jobs, then in 1965, I followed my dream of travelling the world. I started in Canada and worked there for two years, then travelled to Japan and worked there for a year. I met my Japanese girlfriend, and we travelled around SE Asia dodging the Vietnam War. After that it the heat, poverty and colour of India, and then the arid land mass of Afghanistan and Iran. Finally, Turkey and Europe. All done on a shoe-string budget.

After England I worked for 6 years in Japan, teaching English, working as a copywriter and journalist. I then moved to Spain and followed my hobby and opened a squash club which I ran for 12 years. Then marriage brought me back to the UK, where I taught and coached Squash and had two children.

Those experiences are behind the stories that I have written, with characters an amalgam of people I knew, and characters created to match the times.

Don't miss out!

Visit the website below and you can sign up to receive emails whenever David Scurlock publishes a new book. There's no charge and no obligation.

https://books2read.com/r/B-A-FNMGB-GRALF

BOOKS 2 READ

Connecting independent readers to independent writers.

Did you love *The Spanish Connection*? Then you should read *The Malacca Umbrella*[1] by David Scurlock!

[2]

The Malacca Umbrella

    Eneko Sora and his partner George's latest case revolves around a hidden ruby, representing immense wealth and power that will determine the future leadership of a region in Borneo. This sets in motion the Sultan's intricate plan to ensure his youngest daughter, Jasmin, inherits his legacy, bypassing his two corrupt elder daughters.

    The Sultan's plan compels his three daughters to embark on a dangerous quest. This quest becomes the focal point of the story's conflict as various parties, driven by greed and ambition, attempt to manipulate the situation for their own gain.

---

1. https://books2read.com/u/bzklvG

2. https://books2read.com/u/bzklvG

Jasmin's sisters employ gangs from London, the "villains from the smoke". Their relentless pursuit of the treasure and willingness to employ violence and intimidation to obtain it creates a constant threat to Eneko, George, and Jasmin.

The protagonists' efforts to protect Jasmin, outsmart their opponents, and ensure the successful execution of the Sultan's plan form the core of the story's action and suspense.

Read more at www.yamapublishing.com.

Also by David Scurlock

The Eneko Sora detective series
The Malacca Umbrella
The Spanish Connection

Standalone
The Missing Samurai Sword

Watch for more at www.yamapublishing.com.

www.ingramcontent.com/pod-product-compliance
Lightning Source LLC
Chambersburg PA
CBHW020150180626
46810CB00004B/1817